*He want*

Despite her initial shock at his bumbled proposal, Darby found that John's words warmed her, touched her in a way she was helpless to explore just then. He was so earnest, so determined that she couldn't help but be drawn to him, long to kiss him.

"John...I think you and I need some time to adjust before either of us says anything we don't mean."

"I don't need time, Darby. I know how I feel. I know what I need to do. And nothing you say is going to stop me."

"We're not teenagers, John. When something like this happens, you don't have to get married."

"Time," he said pensively. "If it's time you want, Darby, then it's time I'm going to give you. But I promise you, no matter how long it takes, you are going to marry me."

Dear Reader,

A rewarding part of any woman's life is talking with friends about important issues. Because of this, we've developed the Readers' Ring, a book club that facilitates discussions of love, life and family. Of course, you'll find all of these topics wrapped up in each Silhouette Special Edition novel! Our featured author for this month's Readers' Ring is newcomer Elissa Ambrose. *Journey of the Heart* (#1506) is a poignant story of true love and survival when the odds are against you. This is a five-tissue story you won't be able to put down!

Susan Mallery delights us with another tale from her HOMETOWN HEARTBREAKERS series. *Good Husband Material* (#1501) begins with two star-crossed lovers and an ill-fated wedding. Years later, they realize their love is as strong as ever! Don't wait to pick up *Cattleman's Honor* (#1502), the second book in Pamela Toth's WINCHESTER BRIDES series. In this book, a divorced single mom comes to Colorado to start a new life—and winds up falling into the arms of a rugged rancher. What a way to go!

Victoria Pade begins her new series, BABY TIMES THREE, with a heartfelt look at unexpected romance, in *Her Baby Secret* (#1503)—in which an independent woman wants to have a child, and after a night of wicked passion with a handsome businessman, her wish comes true! You'll see that there's more than one way to start a family in Christine Flynn's *Suddenly Family* (#1504), in which two single parents who are wary of love find it—with each other! And you'll want to learn the facts in *What a Woman Wants* (#1505), by Tori Carrington. In this tantalizing tale, a beautiful widow discovers she's pregnant with her late husband's best friend's baby!

As you can see, we have nights of passion, reunion romances, babies and heart-thumping emotion packed into each of these special stories from Silhouette Special Edition.

Happy reading!

Karen Taylor Richman
Senior Editor

Please address questions and book requests to:
Silhouette Reader Service
U.S.: 3010 Walden Ave., P.O. Box 1325, Buffalo, NY 14269
Canadian: P.O. Box 609, Fort Erie, Ont. L2A 5X3

# What a Woman Wants

## TORI CARRINGTON

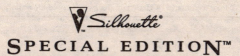

## SPECIAL EDITION™

Published by Silhouette Books

**America's Publisher of Contemporary Romance**

This book is for the real-life heroes who put their lives
on the line every day so that we may live ours.
And for our boys, Tony, Jr. and Tim, our personal heroes.

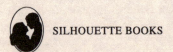 SILHOUETTE BOOKS

ISBN 0-373-24505-X

WHAT A WOMAN WANTS

Copyright © 2002 by Lori and Tony Karayianni

This edition published by arrangement with Harlequin Books S.A.

® and TM are trademarks of Harlequin Books S.A., used under license.
Trademarks indicated with ® are registered in the United States Patent
and Trademark Office, the Canadian Trade Marks Office and in other
countries.

Visit Silhouette at www.eHarlequin.com

Printed in U.S.A.

**Books by Tori Carrington**

Silhouette Special Edition

*Just Eight Months Old...* #1362
*The Woman for Dusty Conrad* #1427
*What a Woman Wants* #1505

## TORI CARRINGTON

is the pseudonym of award-winning husband-and-wife writing team Lori and Tony Karayianni. Twisting the old adage "life is stranger than fiction," they describe their lives as being "better than fiction." Since romance plays such a large role in their personal lives, it's only natural that romance fiction is what they would choose to write in their professional lives. Along with their four cats, they call Toledo, Ohio, home, but travel "home" to Greece as often as possible.

This prolific writing duo also writes for the Harlequin Temptation and Harlequin Blaze lines under the Tori Carrington pseudonym. Lori and Tony love to hear from readers. Write to them at P.O. Box 12271, Toledo, OH 43612 for an autographed bookplate, or visit them on the Web at www.toricarrington.com, www.specialauthors.com or www.eHarlequin.com.

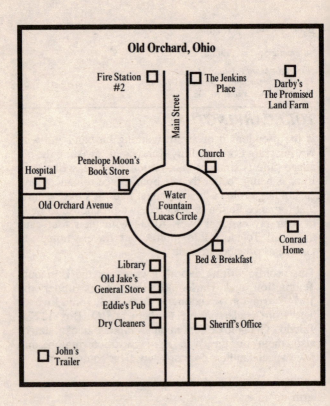

**Old Orchard, Ohio**

Fire Station #2

The Jenkins Place

Darby's The Promised Land Farm

Main Street

Church

Hospital

Penelope Moon's Book Store

Water Fountain
Lucas Circle

Old Orchard Avenue

Conrad Home

Library

Bed & Breakfast

Old Jake's General Store

Eddie's Pub

Dry Cleaners

Sheriff's Office

John's Trailer

## *Chapter One*

*Is this as good as it gets?*

Sheriff John Sparks eyed the holding cells, then closed the outer door with a dull clank. Now *there* was a question. *Is* this as good as it gets? Sure, there were times when he examined his dedication as Old Orchard County Sheriff. Especially recently, with his term up in seven months, reelection around the corner. It was the times when the phone rang at three in the morning that often got to him, summoning him out of bed to see to a domestic dispute over someone's spouse snoring too loud. But there had never really been a reason to apply any major thought to his life and the way he led it. He just lived it. And had been pretty damn happy about it...until recently.

Well, at least he wouldn't have to worry about arguing with anyone over whether or not *he* snored. Simply because there was no one around with whom to argue. He was single and lived alone, and planned to keep it that way. As the youngest in a Roman Catholic family of eight, he'd learned the hard way that large families weren't all they were cracked up to be. Especially when your father considered you a burdensome mistake and your rowdy older brothers and sisters garnered a lot of attention that you might have needed. He felt no need to follow in the footsteps of four married brothers and three sisters, who were all interested in procreating. The thought of a mini-him was more than frightening, it was downright terrifying. But it was the silence more than anything that sold him on the idea of limitless bachelorhood. He liked being able to hear the bathroom faucet drip. To roll over and not have someone's elbow in his nose. To open the refrigerator door and find the bologna right where he'd left it.

It was mornings like now, though, that he knew exactly why he'd taken on the role of sheriff.

John made his way back from the holding cells to the front of the Old Orchard sheriff's office, a one-story brick structure that had been around for nearly a century and had been one of the few buildings spared in the massive downtown fire nearly six months ago.

"Are you sure these are the guys?" George Johnson, the desk sergeant, asked as John handed him the paperwork.

Deputy Cole Parker pushed off from where he'd been leaning against the other side of the counter.

"Of course he's sure they're the guys. He wouldn't have brought them in if he wasn't."

John eyed both men. They couldn't be more different from each other in law enforcement experience. George Johnson had been with the office for more than twenty-five years, some of them good, most of them bad, if you believed what he said. He was used to the laid-back attitude of the former sheriff, who'd retired to a life of fishing and hunting in Montana three years ago, and classified nearly every call that came in as low priority.

On the other hand, Cole Parker—first cousin to one very sexy Darby Parker Conrad—had been hired on to the force in the past three years and was John's right-hand man. He always came into the office earlier than he had to, champing at the bit for more responsibility, more excitement.

"Fingerprints are pretty hard to fake, George," John affirmed as he helped himself to the sludge in the office coffeepot. It tasted as bad as it looked. But seeing as he was just coming off a long night spent out at the abandoned farm on the edge of town, outside corporation limits and in his official jurisdiction, then bringing in the two out-of-state escaped convicts, he'd have knocked back battery acid if it even remotely resembled coffee.

George looked over the paperwork, made a notation, then put the papers aside. "So they were camped out at the old Jenkins place, were they?" He shook his head of thick, disheveled graying hair. "Old Violet Jenkins kicked the bucket what, six months ago? And still nothing's been done with her house."

Something like that, John thought. And the reason it was still vacant was that there were no heirs around to do anything with it. He downed half the coffee. And farms like hers weren't exactly hot properties right now. At least not here. Maybe outside a larger town, within commuting distance. But Old Orchard wasn't exactly a bustling metropolis. Which was just fine with him.

"You suppose it's true what they say?" George asked. "That she had all that money from her husband's life insurance tucked away somewhere in that old place?"

John sighed. Gossip like that had kept them all plenty busy after Violet's passing. The paper had carried a speculative piece headlined "Hidden Treasures?" and the next day every teen within fifty miles was combing through Violet's underwear drawer. Along with a couple of local adults he preferred not to think about right now.

"There was never any proof that there was an insurance policy," he said. "Another one for the urban-myth books. Or suburban. Whichever. Whoever ran that piece in the paper should have been fired."

Cole crossed his arms over his too-buff chest, his gaze almost accusatory. "You know, you should have called me when you found out those two were out there. Going in there without backup wasn't very smart."

"They were asleep. No risk at all." John grinned at the younger man. He knew his welfare wasn't behind Cole's rebuke; it was having been left out that ticked him off. Not much happened in Old Orchard, and the capture of the two felons would probably be on the front page of the town's only paper, the *Old Orchard Chronicle,* for months.

Cole took the FBI poster detailing the two fugitives down from the wall of shame. "Well, this ought to make Bully Wentworth think twice about going up against you in the election."

If anything was capable of knocking the wind out of John's sails, it was mention of Blakely "Bully" Wentworth. They were alike in so many ways. Attended the same schools. Shared the same friends. Yet they couldn't have been more different.

"Wentworth isn't interested in being sheriff," George said. "He just wants to use it as a jumping-off point for bigger and better things down the road." He swore under his breath and said something about opportunists and born politicians. "At least your arresting those two will get him out of the paper for a while."

The arrest of the two felons might even be enough to knock over the pieces cropping up lately about his late best friend, Erick Conrad.

John found it impossible to believe that they were approaching the one-year anniversary of Erick's death, even though the paper had begun running pieces to herald the event ten days ago. The last article had gone into detail about Erick's widow and how Erick had planned to leave Old Orchard until he won the affection of one town native, Darby Parker.

John frowned into his coffee cup, finding the writer's use of the verb "won" curious. Yes, John had at one time been attracted to Darby Parker, but that fact had never been known to anyone but him. Not after he'd found out his best friend had set his sights on her. Then Darby Parker had become Darby Conrad, and she and Erick had had twin girls who were now six. And John hadn't thought of her in romantic terms since.

And Erick? Ultimately he *had* left Old Orchard. Nearly a year ago he'd died fighting a four-alarm blaze, and they'd buried him in the cemetery just outside town limits.

John's throat tightened in mid-swallow, nearly causing him to cough up the scalding liquid.

Okay, so it wasn't that hard to understand why he'd been attracted to Darby Parker Conrad. She'd always been a looker, plain and simple, what with all that curly brown hair, brilliant smile and curvy body. But John had been so used to her being Erick's wife he had never stopped to think about the possibility of her ever being free. He absently rubbed the back of his neck. Given what had happened between the two of them three months ago, he should have stopped and thought about just that.

"Anyway, you going to call the feds and let them know about their two wayward friends back there?" George jerked a thumb toward the holding cells, "or do you want one of us to do it?"

"I'll take care of it."

"I'll get it," Cole said at the same time.

John sighed and ran his hand over the stubble sprouting across his jaw. "Yeah, why don't you do it, Cole."

Cole grinned and headed toward one of the back offices. "I'll get right on it."

George watched him go. "Makes no never mind to me who does it, just so long as it's not me. Less paperwork on this end." George looked at his watch and sighed. "My relief is late. Again." He glanced up as the early-spring-morning sun bounced off a reflective source and through the front window. "Maybe this is him."

John tossed his half-full coffee cup into the garbage, then watched as an old truck pulled up to the curb outside the front window. He knew immediately it wasn't Ed Hanover. Not because of his visual confirmation. More as a result of his instant physical reaction to the woman climbing out of the cab. He felt as if someone had just dumped a handful of Mexican jumping beans into his stomach.

Which was pretty much the way he reacted every time he saw Darby Parker Conrad nowadays.

George's exasperated sigh cracked the silence. "Nope. Not Ed." He squinted, apparently trying to make out who was walking toward the door. His bushy brows budged upward as he did. "I'll be. It's the Widow Conrad."

*The Widow Conrad.* John winced. The words seemed more appropriate for an aging, portly woman who had lived the better part of her life with her mate, not a walking bombshell like Darby, who still had her whole life ahead of her. Yet the unlikely juxtaposition didn't change the fact that she was a bombshell. And that she was a widow. More specifically, his best friend's widow. And even if he couldn't seem to keep that detail in mind whenever he saw Darby, the town did.

George's gaze slid to John. For some inexplicable reason, John had to fight an urge to fidget. "What do you suppose she wants?" George asked.

John couldn't have said anything if he'd tried, but he thought he was doing pretty well at keeping his secret physical reactions…well, a secret. Fact was, he hadn't seen Darby for at least a week, and his body was letting him know that was much too long. Where he'd once gone out of his way to go out to her place to offer his aid and company in the wake of Erick's death, following their spontaneous moments together in her barn three months ago, he'd decided it was best to keep his contact with her to a minimum. And during those times when he did drive the half hour out to her place, he always made sure the twin girls, Erin and Lindy, were around to act as chaperons. Not that it made much difference. He could be up to his armpits in watercolors, the girls chattering a million miles a minute, and he'd get caught up in the way Darby made dinner or fed the myriad animals she took care of, or put together her special mail-order black-and-white photos in handmade frames, or saw to a thousand other mundane chores that left him free to appreciate her with his hungry eyes.

This morning she wore a simple denim jumper over a white T-shirt, a red jacket over both. But there was nothing simple about the way she looked. She looked…well, like a beautiful woman with something on her mind.

* * *

Darby Conrad hesitated outside the county sheriff's office, headed back for the truck where Erin and Lindy sat peering out at her, then stepped back onto the sidewalk again. She should have waited until after she'd taken the twins to school. She should have worn jeans, instead of a dress. While she was at it, she might consider that it wasn't a brilliant idea to come downtown at all.

Straightening a strap on her jumper that needed no straightening, she glanced at her watch. Was it really only 8:00 a.m.? She closed her eyes and took a deep breath.

"You're stalling, Darby. Just go right in, tell John you want…no, need, to talk to him. Tell him the news. Then…"

Her words stopped there. Which wasn't surprising. She hadn't actually gotten beyond the "then" part of the whole situation yet. And there would be a "then." There had to be. Things like this didn't happen without a "then" coming up quickly from behind. But somehow she couldn't seem to come up with one right now. She needed to get this out of the way before she could move onto the "then." She sighed. Erick had always told her she had a one-track mind. She twisted the plain wedding band on her finger, her faint smile all but disappearing. She wondered what Erick would say now….

A horn blew, nearly startling her straight out of her leather clogs. She stared at the truck cab and the two giggling six-year-olds inside. She wagged her finger at them, made sure she had the truck keys in her pocket, then called, ''No breakfast at Jeremy's for you two if you keep it up.''

Darby shook her own head and made a beeline for the front door of the sheriff's office. No one could ever accuse her of being a coward. She'd made it a point to embrace life head-on. That, of course, was before she'd found out how unpredictable, how mystifying, life could be.

She nearly tripped over her own feet. Grimacing, she looked down to find it wasn't her feet she'd tripped over. Rather, a cat, which had zipped inside the door in front of her. A black-and-white scrap of fur she recognized from her countless visits to the fire station.

What was Spot doing over here? She rolled her eyes and allowed the glass door to whoosh shut behind her. She knew John was here. Had seen his SUV parked out front. But that didn't stop her pulse from kicking up when she saw him. Whether it was her growing anxiety or the attraction that seemed to sizzle between them, she couldn't be sure. She suspected both would make her feel jittery, dry-mouthed and self-conscious.

Whether as town bad boy or county sheriff, John Sparks had always had the type of looks that made her knees go weak. But in his jet-black pants and the gray short-sleeved shirt of his uniform, he made her forget what she was thinking about. Aside from his mile-wide grin and his neatly trimmed dark hair, authority and strength seemed to emanate from him. And she knew it was more than just the uniform. He had the same effect on her in jeans and a T-shirt.

"Morning, Darby," George called from behind the counter.

Darby tried for a smile, but failed. "Morning, George." Then to John, "I need to talk to you."

How was that for subtle?

John's grin vanished. Darby curled her fingers into her palms. But oddly it wasn't her hands that dampened but her feet. So much so, she nearly slid out of her shoes.

"Oh." John's simple response might have been meant as a question, but came out as a statement.

Darby nodded. "Can I, um, borrow you for a minute?"

The expression on his face was curious, panicked and all too wary. He gestured toward the counter. "George and I are taking care of some important business. Can it wait?"

Darby looked at the bare counter, considered the relaxed stance both men were in when she'd entered and decided she was being put off.

*Oh,* indeed.

She raised her brows, surprised and stung. John had never put her off before. The possibility that he might hadn't even remotely crossed her mind during the drive into town. She caught herself absently tugging on her dress strap and stopped.

"It's important."

John opened his mouth, but it was George's words that sounded. "Looks like the lady means business. You should hear what she's gotta say, Sparky."

John's grimace didn't detract from his handsomeness, Darby would've thought if she hadn't been so

nervous. He gestured to the glass-enclosed office behind him. "You want to go in there?"

Darby glanced toward the truck parked on the
street. "The girls are outside. I'd really like to stay
where I can keep an eye on them."

John's gaze strayed from hers to the truck. He gave
a halfhearted wave, and she guessed the twins waved
back, judging by John's smile.

"You want to go outside, then?"

She nodded. "Outside. Outside's good."

He got that curious/panicked/wary look again. She
turned and led the way out onto the sidewalk.

It was nearly April, but the ground had yet to catch
up with the new warmth of the air, leaving the mornings chilly. Darby pulled her jacket a little more
tightly around her midsection and looked around the
relatively quiet street. Shops were opening, the church
bell began to chime off the hour, and a couple of
blocks up kids were heading off to school. She waited
for John to follow her out. The closing of the door
told her he had.

Along with the commotion from the direction of
the truck.

"Uncle Sparky!" the twins shouted in unison.

Darby briefly closed her eyes, then opened them to
watch two small bodies catapult toward John's legs,
clutching him as if they hadn't seen him in months,
instead of a week.

John looked startled, then grinned and bent down
to talk to the two animated girls.

Darby stood tensely through a hectic version of
"The Life and Times of Erin and Lindy Conrad,"

then before John could ask a follow-up question, she gripped two skinny shoulders and turned the twins toward where the door to the truck gaped open from their joint escape. "Back to the truck, you guys."

"Aw, Mom," Erin objected, digging her heels in. "Uncle Sparky is our friend, too."

"He's also working," she reminded them.

"Yeah," Lindy supported her mother.

Erin elbowed her sister, then shrugged Darby off when she attempted to hoist her into the truck cab. Instead, after much scrambling and inventive positioning, the six-year-old made it inside and claimed the portion of the seat nearer the passenger window. Darby looked down at Lindy, who raised her arms up as if on cue. She sighed and lifted her inside, then secured their safety belts. "Not a peep, you hear? Or else I take you straight to school with no breakfast."

Lindy made a zipping motion with her hand while Erin grimaced at the unconvincing threat.

Darby closed the door and stood for a brief moment to gather her wits. Judging herself ready, she turned to face John. Then found she wasn't ready at all. He looked so handsome with his hair tousled from where the twins had given him one of their full-head hugs, his grin tugging at something deep inside her.

She finally found her voice.

"Look, John—"

"Darby, I thought—"

They spoke at the same time. Darby smiled and glanced away. Had it really only been a week since she'd last seen him? It felt like several weeks. Months, even. The revelation in and of itself surprised her. When she'd lost Erick...well, she'd never expected to feel attracted to anyone again, ever. Much less such a short time after his death. But what she felt for John transcended mere attraction.

Of course, standing there on Main Street, facing John Sparks, sparked some memories she'd long since buried. Only, back then he'd been a rebellious teen, riding his dirt bike up and down the road, his tight jeans and plain white T-shirt drawing the attention of every female, no matter what her age. He'd been James Dean reincarnated. Well, with dark hair, anyway. And she, along with half the girls her age, had comically sighed after him.

Only there was nothing comical about right now.

"You go first," John finally said.

"No, really, that's okay. I think you should say what you have to say first." *Because what I have to say is going to prevent any further conversation.*

"Okay." He slid his hands into his pants pockets. "What I was going to say is that I thought we decided to, um, let things cool off a bit. You know, after..."

After... Darby was well aware of what he was referring to. But like the "then" quotient, three months ago, neither one of them had seen this particular "after" coming.

She nodded. "We did. Agree, I mean."

"So do you think it's a good idea, then, for you to be coming into town like this and asking to talk to me in front of a motormouth like George?"

Darby glanced into the station to see that George's mouth was indeed running like a well-oiled motor as he spoke on the phone. She looked skyward. "Oh, no."

John's eyes narrowed, but rather than the suspicion such an action would imply, concern warmed the mercurial depths. His eyes seemed to be ever changing. One time green, another time blue. But it was the depth that made her feel she might fall right into them and disappear as she caught him gazing at her when he thought she wasn't looking. Just as he was looking at her now. Or with the flame of passion that had gotten them both into so much trouble and completely threatened a good, no, great friendship.

"Darby? Are you all right?"

He appeared about to touch her. For a moment she wished he would. She'd spent countless nights longing for his touch. Wishing they could go back to that day in the barn and start over again.

In the beginning she'd convinced herself that it was Erick's touch she missed. Erick's grin. Erick's amusing wisecracks. It was only when she gave herself over to her dreams that she realized that somewhere over the past eleven and a half months she had stopped mourning her late husband...and begun lusting after his best friend.

"Darby?"

She looked at him, then said, "John, brace yourself. I'm pregnant with your baby."

## Chapter Two

John had faced many events in his life. As a firefighter, he'd willingly stood in harm's way to put out
dangerous fires. As sheriff for the past four years,
he'd faced countless criminals and had even been shot
in the thigh—although, he wasn't certain the shooting
counted, because it had been an accident. All the
same, he had been shot. And he had found himself in
numerous precarious situations that set his heart to
hammering.

But all of those events combined didn't hold a can-
dle to the shock he felt at Darby's quick, quiet words.

She gazed at him expectantly as the sun rose over
the brick two-story buildings across the street and il-
luminated her in a warm glow, setting her auburn-
kissed brown hair afire.

This couldn't be happening.... It wasn't possible.... There was no way....

Darby was Erick's girl. She'd always been Erick's girl. Then his wife. The mother of his twin girls. Now Erick's widow.

There was no way he'd gotten her pregnant.

Darby held her hand up between them, as if to ward off his words, though he hadn't spoken a single one aloud. He noticed that her slender fingers shook, even as he seemed to be looking at her from some faraway place.

"Don't say anything. I don't want you to. I just...well, I thought you should know."

She began to turn toward her truck.

John squinted after her. That's it? She drives into town, makes him forget every last reason he shouldn't lust after her, tells him she's pregnant, then leaves?

He watched his hand reach out and grasp her arm, halting her, though he had no knowledge of sending the command. "That's not possible."

Darby slowly turned her head to look at him, her large green eyes filled with disappointment. "Trust me, John. It is."

His grip tightened. "I didn't mean...well, you know, that it's not possible. What I meant to say is..." What had he meant to say? That it wasn't possible because he didn't want it to be? That she was Erick's girl, always had been? That now she was Erick's widow and it wasn't possible that he had gotten her pregnant? Or maybe he should tell her that fatherhood was down so low on his priority list it was almost nonexistent?

Given the expression on her face, he suspected it would have been better if he hadn't said anything at all. And he certainly wasn't about to voice the rest of the thought fragments trailing through his mind.

"Are you all right?" he asked.

Darby blinked at him, as if his question was the last she expected to hear. The disappointment eased from her face, although he wasn't certain he was happier with its replacement. She looked…well, as confused as he felt. "I'm fine. Or as well as can be expected, I guess."

Good. That was good. Right? "How?" he asked.

Her brow furrowed.

He swallowed hard. "I don't mean how did it happen. I mean how do you know? Have you been to a doctor?"

She shook her head. "No. I did a couple of those home pregnancy tests. Both came up positive." She glanced down to where his hand still lay against her jacket. "I guess I should have warned you that I have a tendency to get pregnant at the mere *mention* of sex."

John's gaze moved beyond her to the twins, who sat in the truck cab watching them curiously. He remembered when Darby had been pregnant with them. Her condition had been the reason her and Erick's wedding had been moved up six months. Rumor even had it that it was the reason the twosome had married at all.

"I was on birth control, you know, until…"

*Until Erick died.* She didn't need to complete the sentence. They both knew all too well why when there was no reason for her to be on birth control. Or should have been no reason. And he...well, he hadn't exactly thought, hey, I'm going out to Darby's, I'd better take some protection. Somehow he'd always thought that if it came down to it, he'd have enough self-control to protect them both.

"Are they reliable? The tests?" he asked, his voice sounding unfamiliar to his own ears.

"As reliable as can be expected, I guess." Darby cleared her throat. "But they only confirmed what I already suspected." She offered up a small smile. "I've been pregnant before. I know the signs."

John's hand slid from her sleeve, almost as if on its own accord, as the news slowly seeped through his shock.

"Look, John," Darby said quietly. "I didn't come here asking for anything. When I verified the results this morning, I just thought you should be the first to know. I really...um, haven't thought things out beyond that. Not yet."

He scanned her face, trying to make sense out of her words.

"Do the twins know?"

"Oh, dear God, no," she whispered.

The blare of the truck horn made her jump. John swung his gaze to the giggling girls.

Darby blew out a long breath, obviously as anxious about her news as he was. She tucked her hair behind her ear and gestured toward the truck. "The only thing I told the twins was that I'd take them to breakfast this morning." Hope backlit her eyes. "Would you like to join us?"

John took an automatic step backward. The idea of sitting with Darby and her girls for any amount of time knowing she was pregnant with his baby...well, scared him absolutely spitless. "I, um, don't think that's a good idea right now. I..." He glanced over his shoulder, almost surprised to find they were standing outside his office. He supposed he expected to be in some parallel, *other* reality. A place he was unfamiliar with that would take as much getting used to as the situation he was trying to absorb.

"Okay," Darby said. "I understand."

John squinted at her. Could she really be that understanding? Her expression was anxious but soft, no hint of accusation in her eyes, no expectation in her shaky smile. Which made him hate himself all the more.

He laughed humorlessly. "This doesn't seem real somehow, you know? I keep feeling like someone should jump from the shadows and cry, 'Candid Camera!'"

She nodded. "I know."

Only, if anyone leaped from the shadows right now, John was convinced he'd draw his gun and shoot him.

He winced, his thoughts only dancing along the edge of what would happen when the town found out what he'd done.

He glanced first one way, then the other, down the street. Everything moved along much as it should on a weekday in Old Orchard. The shops and buildings that had been destroyed by the Devil's Night fires last October had been rebuilt to their former, old-style glory and warmly reflected the morning sun. People went about their business as much as they normally did, a wave here, a greeting there. No one had a clue that Darby had just ripped the rug of John's life out from under him.

The veracity of his position slammed home when he spotted old Mrs. Noonan slowly crossing the two-lane avenue, heading their way. And if she wasn't bad enough, next to her walked the new pastor, Jonas Noble.

"Good morning, Sheriff Sparks. Morning, Darby," Mrs. Noonan said, drawing to a stop beside them, a gnarled hand tucked into Jonas's arm.

"Hello, Mrs. Noonan. Pastor," John said, reaching up to tip a hat that he'd left inside. He eyed the other man, thinking of the gossip swirling around town about Old Orchard's newest addition. As sheriff, he'd had no fewer than three requests that he check into Noble's background, and he'd refused all of them. As far as he was concerned, keeping to oneself was no crime. Even if there was a somber, almost dangerous look to the pastor, a demeanor his pure black garb and longish dark hair only added to.

"Beautiful morning, isn't it?" Jonas said now, his voice low and even.

Darby smiled but didn't answer. Mrs. Noonan homed in on her. "Is everything all right, Darby?"

Darby blinked. "Pardon me?"

"The girls? The farm? I trust all is well?"

If Darby's nod seemed a little too emphatic, John prayed he was the only one who noticed. "Oh, yes. Everything's fine. Thanks for asking."

Mrs. Noonan smiled. "That's reassuring. Seeing as you're in town so early and standing in front of the sheriff's office talking to our young sheriff…well, I was afraid something might be amiss."

Amiss. Now there was a word, John thought. Something was amiss. But if he had his way, Mrs. Noonan, Pastor Noble and George Johnson would be the last three to know about it.

Darby started backing up toward her truck. "Well, I'd better be going. You know, before the twins decide to leave without me."

John lifted a stiff hand in a wave. "I'll talk to you later, Darby."

She avoided his gaze, concentrating, instead, on Mrs. Noonan and the pastor. "It was good to see you both. Give my best to the women's club, Mrs. Noonan."

"I will, dear."

"Good. Good." Darby backed straight into the truck bed, then turned around and virtually ran to the driver's door. Within moments, the truck was rolling away, a short beep signaling a farewell.

Mrs. Noonan sighed and pulled on the ends of her crocheted sweater. "Pretty girl, our Widow Conrad. Wouldn't you say, Sheriff Sparks?"

John tugged his gaze from the truck's disappearing taillights. "Huh?"

The old woman smiled at him, then bid him a nice day and continued on down the sidewalk, Pastor Jonas Noble at her side.

Darby didn't even have to close her eyes to envision John's reaction to her news. His face seemed to be etched into her corneas, coloring everything she looked at. The sizzling heat his eyes held whenever he looked at her. The way he tilted his head just so in a teasing, cautious way. His full-on grin when he forgot what they were supposed to be and, instead, enjoyed what they were.

Given the sharp turn their lives had taken, what *were* they?

Over the past three months she'd been trying to come to terms with her ability to feel attracted to another man so soon after she'd lost Erick, much less wanting one as much as she had John that day in the barn. She'd scrambled for every possible excuse to explain her aberrant behavior. There was the fact that she craved human contact with someone, anyone, capable of carrying on adult conversation. That she missed her husband's touch and yearned for a man to touch her as he once had. Then throw temporary insanity into the mix, and she figured she had all the bases covered.

The only problem was that her explanations didn't stop her from wanting John. Worse, she yearned to feel his hot mouth on hers, his hands branding her breasts, even more now than before.

And now she was pregnant.

Darby crossed her arms and took a long, calming breath that did nothing to calm her. Absently she found herself wishing John was there with her, was voluntarily facing what she was alone. She caught herself and briefly clamped her eyes shut.

She looked around the cozy, lived-in waiting area

of Dr. Grant Kemper's old Victorian home on the outskirts of town. He ran his practice here, in an airy room off the foyer. Although he'd officially closed up shop and retired a few years ago, Darby could think of no one else to go to. Her regular ob-gyn was out. To be seen even in the vicinity of the central Old Orchard medical complex would set phone lines on fire within a minute of her appearance. She didn't kid herself into thinking she could keep her secret for long. She absently splayed her fingers across the flat expanse of her stomach. Oh, no, her little secret would make itself known in her or his own sweet time. But she needed this quiet time to herself for as long as she could hold on to it, if just for the simple fact that her condition was so unexpected. So life-altering.

She rubbed her brow and glanced toward the still-closed door to her right. To the town she was the poor Widow Conrad, whose firefighter husband died a heroic death nearly twelve months ago, leaving her with two young girls to raise all by her lonesome. But while the well-meaning townsfolk saw her that way, she saw her situation completely differently. She wasn't poor. Not by way of finances, not psychologically. She'd known that every time Erick walked out the door to go to work she might never see him again. She'd accepted it when she'd married him. And while his being ripped from her life had left a gaping hole she had feared would never be refilled, she never once thought her own life was over. Things would just be…different from there on out. She and the twins and the farm and her photographic art. That was how it would be. If sometimes the loneliness she felt deep into the night seemed to reverberate straight through her, if every now and again she felt overwhelmed by the sheer enormity of her responsibilities...well, all single parents felt that way from time to time, didn't they? She saw herself as neither unique nor worthy of pity.

Besides, she had two beautiful girls as a result of her brief time with Erick.

Her fingers stilled against her stomach. And soon she'd have another child to add to the mix. John's child.

"Darby?"

So immersed in her thoughts she hadn't noticed the examining-room door had opened and that Doc Kemp stood there watching her expectantly. She smiled and scrambled to her feet. "Sorry about that. Got lost in thought."

Doc motioned her into the room. With his portly build, bushy gray hair and full beard and mustache, there was a decidedly Santa Claus-esque look to him she found appealing. Darby entered the room and he left the door open. She darted to it, looked out into the empty waiting area, then softly closed it.

"Ah. I remember you doing something similar a while back," Doc said. "Approximately seven years ago."

Darby realized he was right. She had done exactly the same thing when she'd feared she was pregnant with the twins.

"Same reason?" he asked.

Darby blinked, looking over the gleaming, precisely placed instruments on a snow-white towel on a countertop that ran the length of one wall. The neatness of the sheet that covered the black leather examining table. The room smelled of disinfectant and somehow made Darby feel safe. She released a long breath, unaware she'd been holding it until that very moment. She laughed quietly. "Yes, I'm afraid so."

If the doctor's eyes widened ever so slightly, if he looked momentarily puzzled, he didn't let on. He merely turned toward a cabinet, took out a kit similar to the over-the-counter ones she'd used herself at home that morning, then motioned toward the connecting bathroom.

Half an hour later, following a pelvic exam and the urine test he'd given her, Darby sat fully clothed on the examining table, feeling an odd mixture of relief and anxiety. Calmed that she'd come to the only person in Old Orchard who wouldn't judge her. And about ready to jump out of her skin at the thought of her suspicions being confirmed. For once they were, there was no going back. No hoping that she'd been way off base, that the two tests she'd done that morning could be wrong, that she wasn't pregnant, even though everything she felt flew directly in the face of those hopes.

Doc came back into the room from where he'd left her alone to get dressed and rolled his stool over toward the table. He smiled at her. "Three months along is about my guess."

Darby didn't have to guess. She knew exactly the moment the baby within her was conceived. And not only because it was the only time since she'd lost her husband that she'd been intimate with anyone, but because being intimate with John had shaken her to the core, awakened myriad emotions, longings that no self-respecting widow with two young daughters should be feeling.

Even so, Doc's word gave birth to yet another unfamiliar emotion. Joy. Simple joy that her special yet brief time with John had resulted in a baby that would forever be a part of her life. Even though she feared John wouldn't. A completely selfish feeling she couldn't help herself from embracing.

"There, there now," Doc said softly, urging a tissue into her hands. Only then did Darby realize her eyes had welled over with tears. "If I recall, you had the exact same reaction when you found out the twins were on the way. And look at where you and they are now. It wasn't the end of the world, was it?"

She managed little more than a shake of her head. She couldn't even attempt to tell him that her tears were as much out of joy as sorrow.

Doc Kemp reached out and rested a liver-spotted hand on her knee. "You've been through a lot in the past year, Darby. I won't lie to you, I'm a little surprised to see you here, sitting on my examining table again after so long, facing the same problem, but I'm the last person to judge anyone on their actions." His expression grew solemn. "But you don't have to do this alone, you know. We're all here for you."

Darby put her hand over his. "Thanks, Doc. Unfortunately not everyone's as understanding as you are."

"Maybe not. But they're not all that bad, either."

"Maybe."

She wished she could be as convinced as Doc. She'd learned long ago that people liked to fit you into a certain, predictable mold. Should you break free of that mold, step outside that neat little box, judgment could be swift and unkind. The same townsfolk who continued to help her around the farm, showing up on her doorstep with tools in hand determined to assist her through her loss, might all turn in the other direction, leaving her alone. Where now they whispered, "That's the poor Conrad widow. Awful, the way she lost her husband and those poor kids their father," when they found out she was pregnant they might say, "Not even a year since her husband died. The world's going to hell in a handbasket and that one is hurrying it along."

She wouldn't even consider what they would say when they found out her late husband's best friend was the baby's father....

"A baby," she whispered.

Doc patted her knee again, then removed his hand.

"I can't quite bring myself to believe it." She ran her damp palms over the denim of her dress.

Doc nodded. "Babies are known to have that impact on people."

He rolled his stool over to the counter, swiftly wrote something down on a pad, then scribbled something on the back of one of his business cards. "You'll probably want to consult with your own ob-gyn when you're ready?"

"Yes."

He smiled and handed her a prescription. "This is for vitamins."

She glanced at what he'd written and said, "I've already been taking them."

"Good girl." He pressed the other card into her hand. "I'm heading out to Myrtle Beach tomorrow. This is the number I'll be at." He curved his hand around hers. "If you need anything, anything at all, call me."

"I will," she said quietly, although she knew that she wouldn't. She'd already asked too much of him. No, what she had to face, she had to face alone. Correction, she and her small family would face, together.

From the other room, the front door slammed, followed almost instantaneously by the opening of the examining-room door. Darby gave a start, then found herself staring straight into Tucker O'Neill's face. She wasn't sure who was more surprised. Then quickly decided he was the more surprised. While he had no reason to expect her to be there, she knew he'd been staying at Doc Kemp's place for some time now. A doctor himself, he'd opted not to follow in his mentor's footsteps and instead, took great pleasure in working in the emergency department at the county hospital.

Doc Kemp frowned at him. "I've always told you you needed to learn some manners, Tuck."

The younger man barely seemed to register the gibe. "I didn't know you'd hung the shingle back out, Doc."

Darby watched Doc shift the file he'd made for her into a drawer, then close it. He turned to face them.

"I haven't. This is a personal visit. Isn't that right, Darby?"

She nodded and forced a smile. "Personal."

"And even if it weren't," Doc said, "whatever happens in this house is strictly confidential. Isn't it, Tuck?"

Darby felt suddenly as if the topic had moved beyond her to something that existed between the two men. Especially when Tuck grimaced. "I'll be back in a while."

Just as quickly as the door had opened to let Tuck in, it closed on his departure, leaving Darby once again alone with Doc. She slumped and groaned.

Doc crossed to stand in front of her, a reassuring smile on his grandfatherly face. "What Tuck does or doesn't suspect is not what's important right now, Darby. Remember that. I'll see that he doesn't go shooting his mouth off where he shouldn't."

She looked into his eyes, wanting to feel at ease with his reassurance, but unable to. "I appreciate it."

He squeezed her shoulder.


A king. A man in charge of his domain. All-powerful, all-knowing. That was how Sheriff John Sparks usually felt when seated in his office. He dropped the telephone receiver back into its cradle, then pushed the paperwork in front of him aside. Okay, so maybe he only felt like that sometimes. When he was alone, took a deep breath and allowed his more fundamental side to step out from the shadows. But he never indulged the emotions for more than a few moments. Never longer than it took him to square his shoulders, puff out his chest and quell the desire to beat his chest like Tarzan.

He fingered the papers needed to transfer the federal prisoners back where they belonged. Of course, right now he felt like the film that coated the bottom of his shoes. Like Judas for betraying his best friend. Like a heel for treating Darby as if she'd just told him she was coming into town to buy some new tires, not tell him she was pregnant.

Good God.

Just thinking the words made his gut twist into knots.

Pregnant.

Baby.

Mother.

Father.

*Holy cow.*

Propping his elbows on his desktop, John scrubbed his face with his hands.

First in community college law-enforcement classes, then at the fire-department academy, he'd learned how to save lives, protect lives, even take a life if it came down to it. But never in his thirty years had anyone ever talked to him about creating a life.

He grimaced. Okay, there was the botched attempt his father had made when he was ten. It had been all John could do not to laugh as Walter Sparks had awkwardly paced in front of him, where he sat on the bottom bunk in the room he shared with Ben, reciting a speech John was sure he'd used at least four other times with his older brothers. Remembering it now, he thought that with eight kids of his own, his father should have been a pro at relating just how children came into being. But he hadn't been. Most of John's knowledge about sex had come from his older siblings and his peers.

And the greatest lesson he'd learned had come from Erick. When you got a woman pregnant, you married her.

Something brushed against his leg and he started. He pushed his chair back to stare at the black-and-white firehouse cat. "What do you want, Spot?"

If one was to believe the stories circulating around town about the feline that thought she was a dog, she had a habit of showing up on the doorsteps of those most in need of help, no fires necessary. And it was there she stayed, seemingly for no reason at all. Then, when the crisis went away, so did the cat.

Dusty Conrad's wife, Jolie, believed the stories. She even credited the cat for helping to bring her and Dusty back together last autumn.

Of course John didn't buy into any of the stories. Not even Jolie's, although Jolie was one of the most levelheaded people he knew. He patted the cat on the head, then scooted it toward the door before his allergies kicked in. "Go on now. Why don't you go see what ol' Ed has for you." He gestured toward the door and the counter behind, where Ed Hanover had taken over for George Johnson. Ed was always eating something or other.

John absently plucked the papers from his desk, read the fax number he'd been given over the phone, then dialed it and laid the papers in the document holder.

He imagined what his father might say at the news that his youngest had gotten a ''good'' girl pregnant. He could practically envision him tucking in his shirt, hiking up the waist of his slacks and then saying, ''a Sparks always lives up to his responsibilities.''

Of course his many memories of his father saying that had come as a result of some minor infraction such as Ben's being an hour late delivering his newspapers. Or his own promise to shovel the neighbor's walk in the dead of winter. Certainly nothing that even neared the magnitude of this.

Still, his father's words made a lot of sense. Had he planned on being a father? Unequivocally, no. Did that change things one iota? Again, no.

He leaned back in his chair, rocking slightly. Well, then, it only stood to reason that this particular Sparks should live up to his responsibilities, didn't it?

He sprung from his chair as though it had catapulted him. No way. He couldn't believe he was even contemplating such an option. No, not an option. It didn't even near possibility status, as far as he was concerned.

He paced one way, then the other, but stopped when he caught himself tucking in his short-sleeved shirt and hiking up his pants.

What would Darby expect him to do?

The mere thought of her made his stomach pitch toward his feet. Not because she was pregnant, although that detail didn't exactly have a small impact on him. No. Just thinking of her made him long for something he'd never known he wanted. Something he couldn't quite define. Filled him with an unnamable something that made him want to hop in his SUV and head straight out to her house.

He decided to do just that.

Pressing the button to forward his calls to his cell phone and plucking his hat from the desktop, he headed for the door. He still didn't have a clue about what he was going to do or say. But he suspected he'd figure it out by the time he got there.

## Chapter Three

The four-bedroom farmhouse on the outskirts of town sat nestled in the middle of the Promised Land Farm, 150 acres of ripe farmland that had just been plowed and planted. Having been raised in an apartment over the Laundromat in downtown Old Orchard, Darby usually took great satisfaction in her home, her surroundings, living the life she'd always longed to but never had until she married Erick.

Right now, however, she just wished the world would stop spinning for thirty seconds.

No, ten. That was all she needed. Just enough time to find the patience she usually had for the people who tried to help her out since Erick's death but somehow managed to make life even more of a challenge.

She'd returned home after her doctor's appointment to find that the teenage girl from up the road had left the pen gate open when she'd fed the animals. Everything from a llama to a miniature horse was left trampling all over the crooked rows of corn Old Man McCreary had planted last week. And now Erin had let Billy the Goat into the kitchen, the dinner potatoes were boiling over, Lindy was on Darby's heels with nonstop questions, and somewhere in the house the cordless phone was ringing, even though Darby couldn't for the life of her remember where she'd left it.

"Mom, do babies really come from mommies' stomachs?" Lindy's latest question nearly sent Darby skidding across the tile as she tried to keep Billy from devouring the blue-and-white checkered tablecloth. She tugged on the full-grown goat's collar, and he in turn tugged on the tablecloth, sending the dinner placements crashing to the floor.

Darby sighed, nearly backing into Lindy. "Yes, sweetie, babies really do come from mommies' stomachs."

She swallowed hard. There wasn't even a remote chance that her six-year-old daughter was talking about her own mommy, or the brother or sister who was on the way.

She tousled the girl's blond curls as she bent over to retrieve the plastic cups. She'd learned long ago that while plastic might not be the most refined choice, it was the most practical. And the latest mishap only served to prove the point.

"But..." Lindy began.

Darby began stacking the plates and gathering the silverware, then leaned over and switched off the heat under the pan of potatoes. "Lindy, you remember when Petunia had her colt last year, don't you?"

From the corner, where Erin was ineffectually pulling on Billy's lead, came a laugh. Then Lindy said, "Mom, Petunia's baby came out of her butt."

Darby snapped upright, finding the imagery on top of everything else a little much. She wasn't going to touch that one with a ten-foot pole. The girls were six. She'd explained where babies come from when Petunia gave birth and wasn't quite up to another run-through just now. Not considering she'd be coming awfully close to describing the circumstances that had led to her own current pregnancy.

"It did not come out of her butt, stupid," Erin said, giving up trying to control the goat and planting her hands on her hips.

"What did we agree about name-calling, Erin?" Darby asked.

"Dummy," Lindy said to her sister, then stuck out her tongue.

Darby put her hand on Lindy's head and turned her in the other direction. "Go see if you can find the phone before it stops ringing, okay?" As soon as one twin was out of the room, she turned to the other. Completely oblivious to her mother, Erin opened the back door and gave Billy a swift kick to the hind leg. The goat brayed and darted outside.

"Erin!" Darby gasped, appalled at her daughter's actions.

"Whoa there, buddy," a male voice sounded.

Darby's heart hiccupped as she waited for the visitor to show himself. A second later, John's hesitantly smiling face appeared on the other side of the screen.

"Hi," he said.

Hi, indeed. Amidst the chaos swirling around Darby, just looking at John standing there, crisp and fresh in his sheriff's uniform, his hair neat, his chin shaved, his grin warm and sexy, made her feel a different kind of chaos swirl inside of her. He looked better than any one man had a right to. Always had. But now that she'd not only been intimate with him but carried his child, she felt a connection that bound them as surely as the attraction that hummed between them.

"Um, hi," Darby managed, hoping her smile wasn't silly or too revealing. But so what if it was? She was glad to see him.

She watched his hazel eyes water. He turned his head, then sneezed.

Allergies. The goat…

Erin soundly closed the door in John's face even as he murmured a "Pardon me" for the sneeze.

"Erin!" Horrified, Darby stared at her daughter. First the kick to the goat, then slamming the door on John. What had gotten into the girl? While Erin's tongue could be sharper than a rapier, Darby had never known her daughter to be cruel to any of the animals, and she'd certainly never displayed anything but adoration for her "Uncle Sparky," a title bestowed on John before the girls could even walk. Just that morning she'd flung herself at him as if he were king of the world. What had happened to change that?

Darby hurried to the door, nearly tripping over Lindy as she came rushing in from the other room, the cordless phone in her hand.

"It's Aunt Jolie, Mama."

"Thanks, sweetie." Darby took the phone, then opened the door. John still stood there, his shocked expression likely mirroring her own. "I'm so sorry, John. Come. Come in."

Darby moved from the door and whispered to Erin, "That was very rude. Apologize."

Erin stuck out her bottom lip, stalked to the kitchen table and plopped down in her chair. Darby gave John an apologetic look. "I'll be with you in just a moment." She lifted the receiver to her ear. "Hi, Jolie. Is it all right if I call you back?"

Her best friend and sister-in-law's quiet laughter told her she'd overheard. "Sure thing. Sounds like you've got your hands full."

"Understatement. Thanks, Jol. Talk to you later."

She pressed the disconnect button, then curled her arms until she held the phone against her chest. "Hi, again," she said to John.

If her voice sounded a little breathless, that was normal, wasn't it? Considering the past hour and all that it encompassed? It didn't have to mean that just looking at John made shivers rush over her skin or her toes curl in her clogs.

His grin only heightened her reaction.

Darby jumped at the sound of a thud, making her realize she'd been staring. She glanced at where Erin had set a glass down hard on the table, finishing the place settings with Lindy's quiet help. Then the sulky six-year-old pushed the fourth chair to the corner and put a laundry basket full of clean clothes on top of it. Darby realized her daughter was attempting to circumvent any intentions Darby might have of inviting John to dinner. Just what had happened when she wasn't looking to make her feel such animosity toward John?

He cleared his throat, the sound filling the quiet room. "I, um, didn't think that it was dinnertime. Maybe I should come back later," he said, apparently not missing Erin's actions, either.

"No," Darby said quickly. A little too quickly. Movement caught her eye, and she stared at the cat that had nearly tripped her that morning outside John's office. What was Spot doing all the way out here? She smiled at John. "I mean, you know there's no such thing as a wrong time to drop in. Here—" she cast a warning glance at Erin, then pulled out her own chair "—have a seat. Would you like some coffee or something? And of course you'll have to stay for dinner."

John sat down. Behind him, Darby ignored Erin's openmouthed, aghast reaction even as the girl picked Spot up. "Sorry, but I can't—stay for dinner, that is. I'm on call tonight and should stick a little closer to town." He cleared his throat. "Can we talk? You know, for a couple of minutes?"

Darby nodded as she drained the water from the potatoes. "Sure."

"I was hoping we could maybe talk alone?"

"Oh." She looked at the twins. She made a point of including them in everything that went on in the house. Especially since Erick died. Her cheeks flamed as she remembered things in which they weren't welcome to participate. Like her hot-and-bothered tryst with John in the barn three months ago. "Lindy? Erin? Why don't you two go wash up for dinner?"

They raced for the door, obviously intent on completing the chore as quickly as possible. Darby added, "Then pick up your rooms until I call for you, okay?"

"But, Mom—"

"Erin, please. Can you do as I ask just once without questioning me?"

To her surprise, Erin didn't argue. Though her pouty expression didn't disappear, she did do an about-face and leave the room without another word, clutching Spot to her chest.

Darby grasped the back of one of the chairs. "I'm sorry about that. I don't know what's the matter with her today."

"Funny, it's almost like she can't stand the sight of me."

Darby sat down and leaned forward. "Oh, no, that's not it at all. Erin's too young to know whom she likes or dislikes. I think maybe she's feeling a bit...I don't know, threatened by you, that's all."

"I'd never do anything to hurt either of those girls," he said quietly.

She smiled. "I know you wouldn't. And they know that, too. That's not what I meant by 'threatened.' Whenever you come over, you distract me from them. Take my attention. And it hasn't been quite a year yet since..."

She trailed off. If anyone knew when Erick had died, it was the man in front of her.

She looked everywhere but at his face. "Anyway, I'm sure Erin's just having a bad day. We're all known to have one every now and again. She'll probably be back to her old friendly self before we know it."

At least she hoped so. It was going to be hard enough for her to handle what she was facing without a rebellious child on her hands.

She took a deep breath and smiled at John again, finding that the mere act of doing so made her feel a thousand times better. "So…what's so all-fired important that you need to talk to me alone?"

He shifted, looking doubly uncomfortable. Darby's gaze dropped to where he juggled something in his hands. Her eyes widened. She'd been so distracted when he'd come in, she hadn't noticed he was holding anything, much less the bouquet of wildflowers, a red foil-wrapped package of chocolates…and a suspicious, small jeweler's box.

A lump the size of a potato clogged her throat. Even as she wondered what he was doing with the items, it registered that the gifts might be the cause of Erin's behavior. In one glance, Uncle Sparky had transformed into someone interested in taking her daddy's place.

"John?" Darby said slowly, "What are you—"

She gasped as he leaned forward and wrapped his free hand around hers.

"Darby, I…I, um, know I wasn't exactly coherent when you told me the news this morning," he said, his thumb setting fire to her skin as he stroked it. "Truth is, you could have knocked me over with a feather."

"John, I—"

"No, please. Let me say my piece."

Darby bit hard on her bottom lip and nodded, trying not to notice how handsomely earnest he looked.

"What I'm trying to say is that if I looked less than happy about the news, it's only because of the surprise factor. You're a great woman. Wonderful. And it's no secret that we have...feelings for each other."

*Oh, God.*

"I think...no, I want..."

Darby stared at him, completely spellbound. Her mouth refused to work. Her heart beat so loudly in her ears she barely heard him.

"Aw, hell, Darby, will you marry me?"

## Chapter Four

"No!"

John winced away from Darby's gasp. She looked like someone had just turned a fire hose on her and was desperately searching for a way to dodge the spray.

Yet somehow she was still one of the most beautiful women he'd ever laid eyes on. Her green eyes were wide and compassionate, her mouth built for kissing for hours on end, her body made for the kind of loving he couldn't stop thinking about wanting to give her.

When he'd decided to come out here, he hadn't known what he was going to do. Okay, maybe he'd known. The flowers and the ring were evidence of that. Only, he hadn't known whether he would have the guts to do it. Proposing marriage was so foreign, the idea alone was enough to strike fear deep into his heart. But when he'd said the words, he'd immediately known they were the right ones to say. They felt right. Darby was pregnant with his child. He was going to do the right thing and marry her.

He'd never imagined she'd say no.

John cleared his throat, for the life of him not knowing what to say now.

He did his best, though, along with a grin that missed the mark. "Well, that certainly didn't come out the way I meant for it to, did it?" he spoke more to himself than to her, finding the house suddenly quiet. Too quiet. Somewhere two six-year-old girls were probably listening with their little ears pressed to the wall. "I've surprised you."

Darby blinked several times, then smiled in a way he could only classify as uncertain. "Umm, I think 'shocked' is more the word I'd use."

A roughly cut flower stem bit into John's palm. He looked down at the bouquet. He'd told Janice at the recently rebuilt General Store that he was picking up the flowers for his mother. It was only after the impulse buy that he realized Janice would probably say something to Mona, then Mona would talk to his mother's best friend, Beatrice, and before the day's end everyone would figure out he hadn't bought the flowers for his mother, but had, in fact, purchased them for someone else.

But he hadn't been thinking about that at the time. He knew how much Darby liked daisies, and he'd wanted to buy her these, no matter the consequences.

And she didn't even appear to notice them.

"Won't these things die or something if you don't put them in water?" he asked, breaking the silence.

Darby merely blinked at him again, not having moved more than that since the moment he'd blurted out his question.

He shrugged, going for nonchalance, but probably looking like an idiot. "Be a shame to have to throw such pretty flowers away."

Finally Darby seemed to snap out of whatever trance she'd gone into. She snatched the flowers from his hand and put them on the opposite end of the table. "Forget about the flowers, John. I want you to, um, tell me that you didn't just ask what I think you asked."

He winced. Her words were like a punch to the gut. No-nonsense Darby. She'd earned the nickname while they were still in college. No matter what was going on, you could count on her to tell it like it was, no-holds-barred. He'd never wished otherwise—until now.

Okay, so maybe he'd mucked up the proposal. But he never thought she'd respond the way she had. He searched her eyes, finding in their depths confusion, a smear of sadness he'd become all too familiar with after Erick's death, and a light that drew him in farther, deeper. He'd always been able to talk to Darby. Always. Yet the prospect of discussing his reasons behind his proposal now seemed impossible.

"But I did. Because it's the right thing to do," he said finally.

The light vanished from her eyes, leaving only the sadness and confusion. "I see."

John cursed himself. Maybe he hadn't done this right. Maybe he should have gotten down on one knee, as he had planned, instead of just blurting out the question like that. There seemed to be some sort of magic involved when guys did that.

He pushed from the table and bent down on one knee, his heart threatening to beat straight through the wall of his chest.

"John!" she whispered urgently, her gaze darting around the room. "What are you doing? Get up!"

He shook his head and reached for her hands, but she tugged them out of reach. He reached farther and caught them in his fingers. Her hands were warm, her palms as damp as his were. It was all he could do not to forget what he'd been about to do in order to marvel at her soft skin. He settled for turning her hands over and rubbing his thumb along the length of her palms. He only half registered her shiver.

"Darby, I...I know neither one of us planned... well, you know." She glanced away. He caught her chin in his fingers and coaxed her to look back at him. "But facts are facts, and things being as they are, I think it would be a good idea if you and I became..."

He nearly said "husband and wife," but somewhere between his lungs and his mouth the words got lost. He stared at her, trying to think of her as his wife. The only wife Darby had been was Erick's.

"I think it would be a good idea if you and I got

married,'' he finally finished. He straightened his shoulders, trying to ignore the sudden itching of his nose.

''Oh, John,'' she whispered, no longer trying to tug her hands away. But the words weren't said in a wistful, happy way, as he'd hoped. Rather, Darby was looking at him as if he was in his Sunday best and had just fallen headfirst into a mud puddle.

Whoa, rejection. He didn't have much experience in that department. In fact, he didn't have any at all.

This time, he was the one to do the hand tugging. She held fast.

Darby leaned closer to him, but John refused to look at her for fear of what he'd find there. ''Is this what you thought I was looking for when I told you...what I did this morning?''

He grimaced. Her gaze traveled over his face, then she ran her fingertips over his hair. A soft smile tilted her full mouth.

''It's the right thing to do,'' he said, damning his allergies to all her animals as he gave in and rubbed his nose against the uniform of his shirt to ward off a sneeze.

She shook her head, disturbing her auburn curls. ''It's completely the wrong thing to do,'' she whispered. ''You don't want to marry me, John. You don't want to marry anyone.''

He opened his mouth to say all that had changed, that it no longer mattered what he wanted, but she lay a finger across his lips to stop him. He nearly groaned at the feel of her flesh against his flesh. That so simple a touch sent his hormones to raging should have concerned him. But he couldn't think much of anything at the moment.

''Thank you, though,'' she said quietly, her gaze dropping to his chest where her fingers ran over the starched material of his shirt. ''I think it's really sweet, you know, that you asked.''

Heat fanned over his skin. ''I wasn't exactly going for sweet,'' he said, his voice sounding much too gravelly.

The hint of a smile turned into a smile. ''I know. And that's what makes it even sweeter.''

Her hand dipped millimeters lower to touch his stomach. He drew a harsh breath and caught her fingers. ''You know, I'm not used to taking no for an answer, Darby.''

Her smile faded.

''I believe marrying you is the right thing to do and I'm not going to give up until I see you and me at that altar.''

Darby's breath snagged in her throat. The material under her fingertips was silky and inviting. John's eyes held a resolution that touched her to her toes.

*He wants to marry me.*

Despite her initial shock at his bumbled proposal, Darby found that his words warmed her, touched her in a way she was helpless to explore just then. He was so earnest, so determined that she couldn't help but be drawn to him, long to kiss him, if not for the panic swirling through her bloodstream, along with a thousand other jumbled emotions. Panic caused not by the thought of marrying him, of becoming Mrs. John Sparks, but fear that he was serious. That he intended to take this ridiculous idea of his and run with it.

"John...I think you and I need some time to adjust before either of us says anything we don't mean."

His jaw flexed, making her itch to inch her palm along the strong length of it. To press her mouth there, against his freshly shaved skin and drink in the tangy taste of him at her leisure. "I don't need time, Darby. I know how I feel. I know what I need to do. And nothing you can say is going to change that."

Something tickled her chest from the inside. "We're not teenagers, John. When something like this happens, you don't have to get married. There are alternatives now."

His eyes narrowed.

"No, no, I didn't mean that alternative. I'm going to go through with this."

The relief on his face was so complete even she felt it rush through her body and warm her all over.

"Time," he said pensively. "If it's time you want, Darby, then it's time I'm going to give you. But I promise you, no matter how long it takes, you are going to marry me."

"No!"

Darby stared at him as if *he* had made the vehement announcement. Because if there was one thing she was sure of, *she* hadn't said the word. Her heart was too busy doing a silly little dance for her to have responded in any manner.

Reality sank in and every one of her muscles went on alert. If the word hadn't come from her or John, who had said it? She wasn't sure she wanted to find out.

She pried her gaze from John's sincere face to find Erin standing in the kitchen doorway. Her tiny frame was tense and battle-ready, her angelic face drawn and tight. Both hands were curled into fists at her sides and she shook as she repeated the word, as if the entire farm outside hadn't heard her the first time. The passion behind her exclamation made the hair on Darby's arm stand on end, made her stomach squeeze ominously. Extricating her hands from John's, she somehow managed to stumble to her feet, and then wondered why the floor suddenly seemed to be swaying. Then she realized that the floor wasn't, she was.

Not a good sign.

"Erin!" she said, her tone one of reprimand. Her gaze darted from her daughter's flushed face to John, who stared at the tablecloth as if afraid it had come alive and was about to smother him.

The six-year-old's entire stance seemed to crackle with electricity as she pointed a stiff finger in John's direction. "You are *not* going to marry him. You're not!"

Of course that had been Darby's own response only minutes ago. But hearing it come from her daughter's young mouth was completely different. Erin's aberrant behavior all day left her drained and confused and just a tad angry.

"Why not?"

As John asked the question, Darby stared at him as if he'd grown another head. He'd lifted his gaze from the table and now stood next to her, looking at Erin with infinite patience.

"Because my daddy's coming back, that's why."

A strangled sound erupted from Darby's throat as every moment of the past year swept through her mind. From that terrible phone call in the middle of the night telling her Erick was dead, to the funeral where she'd clutched the twins to her so tightly she'd been afraid she'd break them, to the here and now and everything that had happened in between. She wouldn't exactly classify the past year as easy. It had been everything but. But she never, ever, would have thought that either one of her daughters would have a doubt about the permanent absence of their father.

"He is coming back. He is," Erin whispered again, moisture sparkling in her wide brown eyes, her crushed expression making Darby feel as if she'd just run over the family dog with her truck. "And that means you can't marry anyone."

Looking much like a rag doll in need of cuddling, Erin turned on her heel and trudged from the room and all the way back up the stairs. Movement nearby drew Darby's attention. She watched as an eerily silent Lindy stepped from the shadows of the living room, her gaze confused and vulnerable as she turned and followed her sister up the stairs.

Darby's stomach roiled ominously. Unlike when she was pregnant with the twins, the first three months of this pregnancy had been so far uneventful.

She had the awful sensation that was about to change.

"Excuse me," she said softly. "I think I'm going to be sick...."

## Chapter Five

Saturday. Usually Darby's favorite day of the week. But as she stood staring out the kitchen window at the rain washing out what had started as a perfectly beautiful spring day, she wondered if the world at large was out to get her.

For some reason, she'd thought time would make losing Erick easier. And it had in some respects. She no longer woke up in the middle of the night, her pillow soaked with tears, her throat sore from sobbing. She'd even finally packed up the last of his clothes and other things and stored them in the attic a couple of months earlier, and placed the silver-framed picture of him that had once sat on her night-stand in the girls' room.

But she would never in a million years have guessed that Erin thought her father was coming back.

She crossed her arms to quell a shiver, remembering the expression on John's face when she'd come out of the downstairs bathroom last night, her teeth freshly brushed, feeling like she'd been hit by a tractor. He had been standing in the same spot she'd left him, looking as shell-shocked as she felt. All in all, she figured yesterday had been a banner day for everyone.

She looked down to find her fingertips rubbing against the inside of her palm. John had been so sweet, so endearing—and so incredibly sexy when he'd dropped to one knee and proposed to her even after she'd already told him no. Not many men would have continued after the first rejection. But he had. She caught herself smiling. With everything happening, she couldn't even begin to classify what she felt for John. Whenever he was within touching distance, she wanted to run her hands all over him. Press her mouth against his if only to stop the ever-present flow of words coming out of it. Feel his hungry, almost reverent touch on her heated skin.

But last night she'd had little choice but to ask him to leave after Erin's heart-stopping display. He'd asked if she needed help, if she'd like him to talk to the six-year-old, but she'd refused the offer, no matter how tempting. It seemed so very long since anyone but her had been responsible for the twins. Still, she watched with her heart in her throat as he gathered his hat and left.

She glanced down at her ring finger and the one item from her time with Erick that she hadn't been able to part with yet. Her simple platinum wedding band. She absently twisted it around and around on her finger, her gaze drawn to the silverware drawer. Hands suddenly shaking, she slid it open. There, under the extra packets of ketchup and mustard she always hoarded when she gave in to the twins' demand for fast food was the small box John had left behind.

Darby's heart dipped low in her chest as she picked up the box and snapped open the lid. She'd been so surprised when he'd sprung it on her last night that she hadn't given the ring more than a cursory glance. There, nestled in the dark-blue velvet, sat the ring he usually wore on his left pinky finger. No sparkling diamond solitaire. No ornate piece of antique jewelry passed down through generations of Sparkses. No, instead, a large tigereye set in thick warm gold drew her touch. She slid the ring out and admired it, curious about the etching on the inside. She squinted for a closer look.

*Erick and John. Best Friends Forever '89.*

Darby's heart jumped as the significance of John's actions clamped around her shoulders. He'd proposed to her with a ring Erick had given him.

"Mom, Lindy says there isn't going to be a picnic today." Erin's voice reverberated through the kitchen. "Tell her it ain't so."

Darby bobbled the ring, positioning herself so the girls couldn't see as she placed the ring inside the box and tucked it back into the drawer. An unsteady smile on her face, she turned to her daughters. "Isn't. The word you want is 'isn't,' Erin," she automatically corrected, relieved she was capable of any response at all.

Erin eyed her suspiciously, an expression that was fast becoming very familiar. Darby bit the inside of her cheek, wondering if it had been wise to leave her talk with her daughter until today, until the picnic they had spent the past ten days planning down to which napkins they would use. Even now the wicker basket was packed full of all the twins' favorites on the counter behind her.

"It's raining," Lindy said unnecessarily.

"That, it is." Darby spared another glance at the drenched day.

"But you promised." Erin crossed her arms in a way that made Darby frown.

"I said it was raining. I didn't say we weren't going to have our picnic." Darby eyed her daughter, waiting for a response.

"But—"

Darby picked up the basket by the handle. "Lindy, you get the blanket. Erin, the pitcher of lemonade is in the refrigerator. Follow me."

Darby led the way up the stairs, watching the girls' faces as they glowered and fought to keep up with her long-legged stride. Within moments, she was in her bedroom, where she had already made some hasty preparations. The daisies John had brought were separated into half a dozen bunches and set around the bed in different-colored plastic glasses. The bird-shaped wind chimes she'd taken from the front porch hung from the ceiling, the gentle turning of the ceiling fan making them tinkle. She'd found a length of green, grasslike indoor-outdoor carpet in a closet that she draped across the bed, and pictures of trees and nature the girls themselves had drawn over the years were pasted on the walls.

"Cool!" Lindy shouted, making a beeline for the bed, the checked blanket still clutched in her arms.

Darby caught her before she could climb onto the mattress. "Wait a minute. You don't want to get grass stains on your new white pants now, do you?"

Lindy giggled as Darby ran her fingers over her plump, little-girl belly, tickling her.

Darby glanced to Erin, who hung back, clutching the pitcher tightly in both hands, staring at the flowers.

"Erin, why don't you put the pitcher down? I'm going to need both of you to help me with this."

Erin slowly did as asked and Darby snapped out the blanket, satisfied when the girls scrambled to the other side of the bed to smooth down the cheery material.

She eyed them across the expanse of the king-size mattress as she switched on the old portable radio on the nightstand. Golden oldies poured out of the small box, filling the room with further warmth. "Okay. Ready, set...go!"

All three of them jumped on top of the bed, rolling around and laughing as if a warm spring breeze was blowing, the birds were chirping and the sun was shining affectionately down on them. As the girls' laughter subsided, Darby drew them to either side of her, squeezing tightly. They so resembled their father with their curly blond hair and big brown eyes it sometimes hurt just looking at them. She pressed a kiss to both their temples, then lay back and sighed.

Somewhere over the past year, through all the grief, the long, pain-filled nights, the struggles to fill the large hole caused by Erick's absence, Darby often felt as if the three of them had become one. One mind. One heart. One body. They hurt and she felt it. They laughed, she laughed with them. They cried, she felt as if the world had been ripped in two.

Now she quietly cleared her throat. "You remember those life lessons I'm always talking about?" she asked, smoothing back their hair. "Well, this is one of them."

Silence. Then Lindy propped herself up on a skinny elbow and looked at her. "What is?"

Darby smiled, then tucked a stubborn curl behind Lindy's ear. "A little rain doesn't have to ruin anyone's parade."

"Parade? That's dumb. There's no parade." Erin rolled her eyes, as if tired of all of her mother's little philosophical tidbits. Tidbits Darby's own mother used to pass on to her when she was younger. The Parker family might not have had a whole heck of a lot of money, but love was never in short supply.

Darby playfully pinched her daughter's wrinkled nose. "It means just because your plans change doesn't mean you can't still work something out. Something fun. Something you'll remember forever."

Erin turned her head away from the contact. "You're not talking about Uncle Sparky, are you?"

Darby fell silent and slowly withdrew her hand. "No. I'm talking about the weather. And life."

Her daughter eyed her warily.

Darby wanted to know just when Erin had turned

so skeptical. When Erick had been around, there was hardly ever a time when either of the twins had anything other than a smile on her face.

Now it seemed that smiles were at a steep premium. And Darby wished she knew the price on the tag.

Spot leaped up on the bed, startling them. They snapped to a sitting position in unison, then laughed, the girls teasing each other over who had been more startled.

Ignoring the cat that had taken up residence in the house since catching a ride over with John yesterday, Darby leaned over the side of the bed, hoisted up the picnic basket and began setting out their carefully planned meals, each one of them different. Pineapple pizza for Lindy. Barbecued chicken for Erin. And a Caesar salad for herself.

She leaned across where Lindy was already making a great attempt at decorating the blanket with fruit and reached for the lemonade.

"I don't think cats and pineapple mix very well, Lindy," she said, her finger brushing what she thought was the side of the pitcher. She turned her head, the smile freezing on her face. She stared at the ornate silver picture frame of her late husband sitting right where it had always sat…until a couple of days ago, when she'd moved it to the girls' room.

A shiver traveled down the length of her arm. She slanted a look at the girls, but they either hadn't noticed her discovery of the picture as they chattered on about how good their food was or were better at playing it cool than Darby feared. A question that wouldn't even have entered her mind a short time ago.

Swallowing hard, she picked up the pitcher and filled each of their uncapped bottles in turn. If she was going to talk to them about John, about his surprising proposal, now was the time to do it. Only how, exactly, did one go about broaching a subject of such a delicate nature?

After the loss of their father, she'd encouraged the girls to talk about their feelings, coaxed them to reminisce about the things they missed most about Erick. She absently smoothed down the front of her blouse, feeling the flat expanse of her belly just below the soft material, and reminded herself that before too long another human being would be joining them. And she owed it to him or her and to John to set things straight with the twins now.

The thought of John made her stomach tighten. Oh, how she wished he were here right now to help her with this.

Her eyes widened a fraction of an inch even as she handed Lindy a napkin. The quiet, subconscious wish was startling. She hadn't wished Erick were there. Or her best friend, Jolie. Or even her mother. It was significant that John's name had surfaced above all the others. And the revelation made her feel more than a bit vulnerable, exposed.

She supposed it might be due to the fact that she was carrying his child. But that excuse didn't ring true somehow.

"Spot!" Erin screamed. "Baaaad cat!"

Darby focused on the scene unfolding around her.

The girls in various stages of devouring their meals. The frisky feline that had pounced on the remainder of Lindy's pineapple pizza, traipsing through the potato salad to do so. One of Erin's drumsticks clutched firmly between her teeth, she leaped to the floor and out the door, mayonnaise pawprints dotting the polished wood floor in her wake.

Darby looked first at Lindy. Then at Erin. Then the three of them gave in to peals of laughter.

John brushed through the sheriff's office door just after 4:00 p.m. and took off his hat. A mini-shower of water landed on the front of his slacks. Great. Not only didn't he have enough sense to get in from out of the rain, now he looked as if his aim in the bathroom department had been off. He wondered what else could possibly happen to make his day any darker. And decided that nothing could make it as dark as last night.

"What's going on?" he asked Ed Hanover, the first-shift desk sergeant.

Seeing as the sheriff's office never closed, John and most of the staff worked alternate weekends to make sure the office was manned at all times. The previous sheriff hadn't seen that as necessary. So during the weekends, the busiest time for any law-enforcement agency, anyone needing help was either directed to the city police or had to track down the sheriff at his favorite watering hole. Most often, the matter had to wait until the following Monday.

The work schedule was the first thing John had

rearranged, much to the chagrin of some of the older workers like Ed.

"Not much," Ed answered in response to John's question.

John tossed Ed his requested dinner from the hot-dog place up the block, along with a couple of meat-loaf dinner trays from a nearby diner for the two prisoners in the back.

"I'll take them the food in a minute." Ed pulled out a couple of French fries and pointed them at him. "You get your Jeep towed out of the mud all right there, Sparky?"

John slid the older man a dark gaze. "Yeah." He hung his rain gear on the rack near the door. "One of the McCreary brothers gave me a line."

Ed stuffed the fries into his mouth, but that didn't stop him from talking. "It can get mighty muddy quick this time of year, what with all the rain we've been getting."

"Yeah," John said again, hoping Ed would get the hint and drop the subject. His run out to the Jones farm to check out a broken window had ended up in his getting stuck in the mud that was the Joneses' driveway. As he'd listened to the account of how the broken attic window had been discovered, he'd been hard put not to tell the young couple that they should consider laying gravel on their driveway. The window? Probably the result of one of the oak-tree branches hitting it during last week's storm, rather than the mischief of the Taylor boys who lived two miles up the road.

Truth was, everything John had attempted to do

that day had ended up a mess. Hell, he might as well go back to yesterday if he wanted an accurate account of just how much could go wrong in one man's life with the utterance of a few earth-shattering words. *I'm pregnant with your baby.*

Ed wiped his mouth with a napkin. "You say something, boss?"

John blinked at him. "What?"

"Nothing. I just thought you mighta said something."

"No, no. I didn't say a word."

And he prayed he hadn't. It was bad enough that Darby's statement echoed nonstop through his muddled, sleep-deprived brain. To have anyone else find out so soon…

The memory of Darby's sweet face when she'd turned down his proposal loomed large in his mind, followed quickly by Erin's vehement response and tears.

He stepped to the call log and glanced through it. Cole was out seeing to a brawl at Harvey's, a biker bar on the outskirts of town. Good. Better the deputy than him. The way things were going, he'd end up backing into the long line of motorcycles and knocking them over like so many chrome dominoes.

Talk about your causes for a brawl.

He rubbed his chin with his fingers, then stared at the dim tan line on his pinky. In the chaos that had surrounded his impromptu proposal the night before, he realized he must have left the ring on Darby's kitchen table. He muttered a curse under his breath.

He hadn't known what he'd been thinking when he

decided to propose. He supposed he expected her to immediately accept. She was pregnant. He had gotten her that way. They got married. Right?

Wrong. He was learning at a rapid rate that things didn't always turn out the way you planned.

"Oh. One of those FBI guys called back," Ed said, finishing his dinner in record time.

John stared at him. "Why didn't you put him through to the radio?"

"You must have been out, um, seeing to the towing of your car. I couldn't reach you." He motioned over his shoulder. "The message is on your desk. He wants you to call him back."

"Fine." John sighed, glad for a reason to leave the room and lock himself in his office. Besides, the sooner he got the two escaped cons out of his holding cell, the better. This was the first time they'd had criminals as dangerous as these guys on the premises. And he'd prefer if the soundness of the cells wasn't tested just now.

"By the way…"

John slowed his step, all too aware of Ed's gossipy opening. He braced his hands against his doorjamb, his back to his co-worker.

"Dusty called for you a few minutes ago."

The "not much" Ed claimed to be going on when John had come in was turning out to be a lot.

"Dusty?" he repeated, cringing when his voice cracked in the middle of the name.

The older brother of his late best friend never called him at work. Lord knew they ran into each other enough at the fire station where Dusty's wife, Jolie, was the chief, and Dusty himself often volunteered after retiring from the department the year before.

"Yeah. Sounded a bit peeved if you ask me. Wanted to know when you'd be back."

*Oh, no. He knows.*

John felt the coffee he'd been knocking back all day begin to churn in his stomach. He opened his mouth to respond, but nothing came out. Not that he would have been heard, anyway. Out front Dusty's red truck squealed to a stop by the curb. He and Ed watched as Dusty got out and stalked toward the door, completely oblivious to the rain running over his brow and down his shirt.

Ed cleared his throat as Dusty nearly yanked the front door off its hinges. "Yep. I'd definitely say he's a little peeved," Ed said.

Those were the last words John heard before Dusty cocked back his arm and socked him right in the eye.

John reeled back against his office door, the glass vibrating threateningly before he managed to grab ahold of the jamb and steady himself.

"Whoa! Just wait a minute here," John said quickly, putting his hand up to stop another onslaught. "Now what did you go and do that for?"

He peered at Dusty and caught his hand before he could land another punch. "Would you stop? I'm on duty, man. Hit me again and I'll have to lock you up in a holding cell until you cool down."

"Just you try it," Dusty ground out, looking like a good twenty minutes of pummeling John's face wouldn't drain a percentage of the anger radiating from him like steam.

"Sheriff?" Ed asked uncertainly behind him. "Shall I arrest him?"

Dusty swung on the older man threateningly as John held his hand up. "No, Ed, that won't be necessary. I'm sure I can take care of this." He stared at his friend even as he checked his right eye for blood. There was none. But already it was starting to swell up and it stung like hell. "I only wish he'd given me a chance to do that before he started throwing punches."

John kicked the door to his office open, then caught it before it could come back and slap him in the other eye. Dusty followed, evidenced by the slamming of the same door. John guessed that before the day was out, the glass would be broken. He removed his firearm and badge and dropped both into a desk drawer, then closed and locked it just in case he was tempted to use either. Then he closed the blinds on the door and windows to block out Ed's curious gaze.

"Tell me it isn't true," Dusty challenged, rainwater drenching his hair and shirt. "Tell me Darby isn't pregnant."

"Okay. It isn't true. She isn't pregnant."

Dusty narrowed his eyes.

"But I'd be lying."

"Why you…" Dusty advanced on him, but during the exchange John had managed to put his big metal desk between them. Dusty stopped just in front of it.

"Hey," John said, holding his hands up. "The last thing I expected to happen was this."

"Tell me about it."

John grimaced and wondered if he should get his gun back out.

But already Dusty's anger was losing some of its steam. He started shaking his head and pacing the office. "I can't believe it. All this time, your going out to the farm, I thought you were just helping Darby out." He turned his stare back on John. "With the farm. Not knocking her up."

John winced at the crude words. "Trust me, it's not exactly what I had in mind, either."

"No?" Dusty asked with a raised brow. "What was on your mind, then? Had you planned to just bang my sister-in-law in secret without any concern for the consequences?"

"As opposed to in public?"

Dusty advanced.

John held up his hand to ward him off. "Whoa. Bad joke." He sighed as Dusty stood his ground. "Anyway, nobody was banging anybody. What happened between me and Darby certainly wasn't planned. And it only happened once."

"Once is all it takes."

"Tell me about it."

Dusty crammed his eyes shut and muttered a string of curses. "What were you thinking? God, I feel like I'm reliving a scene from the past."

John stared at the surface of his desk. No doubt Dusty was referring to the day Erick had told his brother he'd gotten Darby pregnant with the twins before they were married.

"Haven't any of you guys ever heard of condoms? Prophylactics?"

Dusty sank down onto one of the two green metal chairs in front of the desk and ran the heels of his hands over his eyes. John took the opportunity to probe his own injured eye. He winced when pain shafted through his head at the first touch. He didn't have to look into the mirror to know that he was going to have one hell of a shiner.

And it was no less than he deserved. Hell, as long as he was at it, he deserved much worse. He could count himself lucky that Dusty hadn't chained him to the back of his truck and dragged him through town at high speeds wearing a sign that read Condemned Man.

"I just don't get it," Dusty said, and sighed. He leaned back and looked at John through half-lidded eyes. "Jolie and I have been married for six years and can't have a child, while all the single people in Old Orchard get pregnant just looking at each other." He shook his head again. "Life's a bitch."

"You can say that again."

John guessed that was the wrong thing to say, given Dusty's quick glare.

"Speaking of Jolie, how are her and Ellie, any-way?" John asked just as quickly.

"Huh?" Dusty blinked. "Fine. They're fine."

Aside from providing emergency foster care on occasion, Jolie and Dusty had taken in little Eleanor Johansen while her father recuperated from major burns he'd suffered while trying to save his wife from a house fire. As a result of Jolie and Dusty's loving care, Ellie was a healthy five-year-old girl adjusting well to her new circumstances.

"Good. I'm glad everything's going so well," John said.

Dusty's eyes softened, apparently thinking about his family.

John cleared his throat. "If you don't mind my asking, how did you find out about...well, you know?"

"What you want to know is if the gossip is making the rounds, don't you?" Dusty muttered something under his breath. "It wouldn't be less than you deserve, but no. Tuck called me an hour ago with the news. Swore I was the only one he told. Seems he walked in while Doc Kemp was examining Darby."

John nodded, trying not to let his relief be too evident.

"But that doesn't change anything, you know."

"I know." John fiddled with the paperwork on his desk. "You and Jolie—"

"Me and Jolie are me and Jolie," Dusty said, standing again as if the thought of sitting another moment was unthinkable. "What I want to know is when you and Darby are getting married?"

John's throat seemed to completely disappear, leaving nowhere for the saliva gathering in his mouth to go. "What?"

Dusty started pacing again. "You wouldn't have been my first choice as a second husband for my sister-in-law. Hell, I hadn't even thought about Darby's getting married again. But I guess that's neither here nor there now, is it?" He ran his hand over his short-cropped hair.

"We're not getting married."

Before John could blink his one good eye, Dusty had him by the shirtfront, his breath hot on his face. "Pass that by me again?"

Again John wondered if putting the gun away had been such a good idea. "Come on, Dusty, I already asked her. It's the first thing that came to mind when she told me the news." Well, it wasn't exactly the first thing, but Dusty didn't have to know that. "She told me no, flat out. Twice," he added for good measure.

Dusty searched his face, seeming to flinch when he noticed the swelling of John's right eye. "I wouldn't marry your sorry butt, either." He grinned and let him go. "But that's me."

John let out the breath he'd been holding.

"You're going to ask her again of course."

"Of course," John said, although in all honesty, he hadn't gotten that far in his thought processes. He was still stinging from her rejection.

"Good."

And with that, Dusty left the office as quickly as he'd come into it.

John dropped into his chair, wondering how much worse things were going to get. And whether or not he'd survive it.

## Chapter Six

"You promised you wouldn't say anything," Lindy whispered.

Erin crouched in the dark bedroom closet beside Lindy and closed the door. She didn't know why her sister liked the tiny room so much. It smelled musty and damp and the wood floor was hard and cold.

"Say what?" she asked.

Lindy lightly landed a closed fist against Erin's arm. Erin absently rubbed the spot, knowing that if her sister was really upset, she would have hit her harder. "About Dad coming back."

Erin settled down next to her twin and sighed, instantly comforted by the feel of her sister's side against hers. For the past two hours Mom had sat down with them to have one of her heart-to-hearts with them. Tonight's topic had been Dad.

Thank heaven nothing more had been said about Uncle Sparky. But Erin still couldn't help feeling as if she'd just spent the day cleaning out the animal pens. All of them. She yawned so wide her face hurt. Sometimes listening to Mom talk was a hard job.

"I didn't mean to say anything." Erin rested her temple against Lindy's hair and sighed again. "I didn't know what else to do. Uncle Sparky was kneeling on the floor, you know, like we saw in that movie the other day when that man asked that woman to marry him, and Mom was…touching his face." She had a hard time swallowing. What she didn't want to tell her sister was the way her mom had been looking at Uncle Sparky. She'd looked happy, instead of sad. And for a minute Erin had been happy, too. But she knew it was wrong to feel happy. Lindy had told her they wouldn't be happy ever again.

"Where's Grammy?" Lindy asked.

"Where else? Asleep on the chair, one of those romance books open on her chest." She sighed deeply. "I wonder when Mom's going to be home from Aunt Jolie's."

"I wish we could have gone."

"Me, too."

Lindy shifted beside her, switching on a flashlight. The beam flickered and her sister shook it so the batteries would line up again. She stared at the light, wishing for the time when she and her sister used to hide in the closet and play monster with the flashlight Daddy had given them. Then Daddy had gone on his long journey, and real monsters had come out to play.

Lindy fiddled with the walkie-talkie in her hand, her fingers barely fitting around the body of it.

"Here."

Erin took the flashlight.

"Well, hold it steady, dummy."

Erin frowned and used both hands to hold the flashlight straight. Her arms were tired. But her head was even more tired.

Lindy used her free hand to switch on the walkie-talkie, chewing on her bottom lip the way she always did when she concentrated.

Finally the radio hissed and spit like Spot when you accidentally stepped on her tail. Lindy pressed the button to stop the noise.

"Daddy? Come in, Dad. It's Lindy."

Erin's heart beat hard in her chest and her hands got sweaty. The flashlight slipped.

"I said hold it steady!" Lindy whispered over the sound of the radio.

"I am!"

The beam hit the radio and Lindy tried again. "Dad? Daddy? It's me. Lindy. And Erin," she added.

Lindy glared at her and released the button. "He only talks to me."

Erin made a face at her.

The hissing disappeared again. "Dad? Talk to me, Dad. I'm sorry I made you angry with me. Please, please, just say hi."

Erin didn't know why, but it was suddenly hard to breathe, and her heartbeat sounded really loud in her ears. So loud, she wanted to put her hands over them.

"Maybe we need to go somewhere else. You

know, for better 'ception,'' she suggested quietly, hating the sound of the static. "You know, like outside or something."

"Shh." Lindy pushed the button again, her voice sounding funny as she called for their dad again.

Erin shone the light in her sister's face. Tears made her lashes all spiky and her eyes looked huge, just like when they used to play monster. What was even stranger is that she didn't say anything to Erin for shining the light on her.

"Dad? Please, Dad, answer me. I..." A sniffle. "I need you."

Darby had never lied to the girls before. But she tried to convince herself that even she was allowed a little white lie every now and again. Besides, she didn't know how they would react if she'd told them she was going to John's, instead of their aunt's.

The truck hit an especially nasty rut, jarring her teeth as she negotiated the uneven pavement. If she needed any more of an answer, that would be it.

*Somehow word had gotten out.*

Darby's knuckles whitened on the steering wheel as she tried to make out the road in the bouncing headlights. No, not somehow. She knew exactly how word had gotten out. Oh, it had probably started out innocently enough. Tucker O'Neill had accidentally sauntered in on her and Doc Kemper. Doc had given him a warning. Then Tuck had probably, under the strictest of confidences of course, told someone at the hospital while making his rounds. Then that person had secretly told another. And here she was, thirty-six hours later, driving out to John's trailer in the dead of night because her late husband's brother had had it out with the man who'd gotten his widowed sister-in-law pregnant.

Mercy. How complicated things could get so quickly.

She rubbed the furrowed skin between her brows, just thankful her mother had already been over at the house and that she was able to hop into the truck mere moments after Jolie's frantic call explaining the situation. Or as much of the situation as she knew, anyway.

Darby scanned the pitch-black horizon, trying to make out a light, a landmark of any kind. Despite the endless tracks of farmland in northeastern Ohio, this particular road was crowded with thick trees, making her task that much more difficult. She'd never had a need to come out here before now. John's ''poor excuse for a bachelor pad,'' as Erick used to call it, wasn't exactly fit for proper company, she'd heard it told. But when she'd called to see how he was and he'd asked if he could come over to her place, she'd told him that she'd come to him, instead. Then she'd hung up without finding out how he'd fared under Dusty's wrath.

Of course she told herself she should be happy the gossip hadn't yet made the full circuit. If it had, her phone would have been ringing off the hook, and her mother probably wouldn't have let her go until she'd told her everything. She supposed it was altogether possible that Tuck had had an attack of conscience and had given in and called Dusty straight out, instead of the news making it to her brother-in-law via a more circuitous route. She drew a deep breath and held it. Oh, how she hoped that was the case. The last thing she wanted was for the girls to find out from a third-hand source, instead of from their own mother.

She swallowed hard, dreading the moment when she would have to sit them down for that particular heart-to-heart. Her hand slid to her abdomen. A moment that would have to come very soon. A moment that would undoubtedly rank up there as one of the most difficult of her life, if Erin's recent behavior was any indication.

Over a day had passed since John's proposal, and she still hadn't coaxed from the twins the reason behind Erin's bizarre outburst. Not even freshly baked chocolate-chip cookies had been enough to get the two munchkins to talk. They'd just sat on the sofa, their adorable faces blank, and listened while she droned on for so long she got tired of hearing herself. And the more she talked, the more she realized that there was a very good chance that she didn't know her own children as well as she thought she did. Oh, she didn't question their love for her. Or hers for them. But she was coming to see that there were more layers to the twins' personalities than she'd suspected. Something she hadn't noticed, partly because she'd been so busy trying to remake their family into something that didn't include Erick. And mostly because she'd been so determined to heal their wounds she hadn't taken the time to probe and see what might lie underneath them.

Finally a light emerged from the all-encompassing

darkness. Darby leaned forward and squinted at the single bulb hung out on a rough-hewn wooden pole near the road and eased her foot from the gas. Despite how long the drive had seemed to her, John didn't live any farther than fifteen minutes out of town. The only problem was, it was the opposite side of town from where her farm was, making the drive doubly long.

She coasted to a stop next to John's mud-caked Jeep and switched off the engine. The sudden silence made the thud-thud of her heart sound like a jungle drum. She swore that if there was so much as a noticeable scratch on John, she might have to leave a few visible marks of her own on her brother-in-law. What was he thinking, going after John like that, instead of coming to her?

A shadow moved in one of the windows of the one-bedroom trailer and her breath caught.

What had *she* been thinking coming out here?

Her clogs sloshed through the mud that was John's driveway, then clunked on the wood stairs. She lifted her hand to knock when the door was pulled inward and John—one hundred percent sexy hot John—stood looking at her with one of the nastiest shiners she'd ever seen.

"It's not as bad as it looks," John said as Darby stared at him.

"Oh, my God." She lifted a shaking hand to his face.

Suddenly it seemed an effort to even take a breath.

John had spent the past half hour since Darby's

brief phone call pacing the trailer as if it was his first time in it. Now that she was there…well, he wondered if he'd be able to move an inch. He was completely spellbound, watching the myriad emotions cross her beautiful expressive face. First, shock drained the color from her satiny skin. Then her soft brow creased in concern. Then a spark of anger backlit her sexy green eyes. His gaze fastened on her mouth, finding she'd moved even beyond that as the corners of her lush lips tipped up.

"Um, it looks like he really hauled off and popped you one," she whispered, the words sexy despite their meaning.

She seemed to realize that her fingers still lightly probed the area around his eye and awkwardly withdrew them.

John instantly missed her touch. "Yeah. If I'd seen it coming, I could've at least ducked."

Pain erased all other emotion from Darby's face. "Oh, John, I'm so sorry. I don't know how…I mean, I didn't think…" She briefly closed her eyes, then opened them again. John watched, transfixed as the velvet black of her pupils adjusted. "I'm going to kill Tuck."

John realized they were still standing in the open doorway, him inside, her out. He forced himself to step back to allow her entrance. "It's chilly out. Come in."

"Um…okay." Her actions mirrored her words as she hesitantly stepped forward, her gaze taking everything in.

John had never felt so exposed. The only other

women who'd been in his trailer were his mother and sisters. Not even when he occasionally went out did he bring a date back here. There was the distance issue. But mostly he'd never felt moved to invite a woman over.

And having Darby there now seemed...strange, somehow. When he thought of her, he thought of the farmhouse. Her with her slender hands in the fertile earth. Running her fingers over animals as she groomed them. Putting together her mail-order specialty frames of pictures she'd taken herself. Picking up one or the other of the twins.

Now the image that flicked into his mind was of her stretched across the sheets on his water bed in the back bedroom, as naked as the day she was born.

He cleared his throat and motioned toward the brown leather sofa. "Have a seat," he suggested as he headed in the opposite direction, toward the tiny but neat kitchen and away from her. "Would you like some coffee?"

She hadn't budged from where she still stood near the door. "No. I think I'll pass. Thanks."

"A beer? A soda? How about some cocoa? I think I have some of those packet things around somewhere."

Her gaze briefly met his. She smiled, the tiny gesture hitting him squarely in the solar plexus. "You're not going to stop until I have something, are you? Okay, water. Please."

"Water." He pried his gaze from her enchanting face and looked for a glass, noticing from the corner of his eye that she moved toward his recliner, instead of the couch. He grabbed a beer for himself from out of the fridge, then handed her the water.

"Thank you."

He hummed his response and sat on the edge of the couch. When the movement put his knees in direct contact with hers, they both jumped. He moved a little farther down.

"So tell me what happened," she said quietly.

A simple enough question. Only, John had to search his brain for what she could be talking about. Oh! Dusty.

He shrugged. "No big thing. Dusty heard...well, the news that you're...with child...."

She smiled and lowered her eyes.

"Um, namely, my child, and decided he had a few issues to work out with me."

"With his fists?"

"One fist."

"To the eye."

"That's about the extent of it."

She searched the eye in question. "Does it hurt?"

He shrugged. It had hurt like nobody's business only a short time ago. But right now he couldn't seem to think beyond the hammering of his pulse and the simmering heat of need thrumming through his veins. "Not much."

"Did you put something cold on it? A frozen bag of peas does wonders."

Peas? "I have a cold pack."

"Oh. Good."

Conversation evaporated like rain on a hot day.

For a guy who could make conversation with anyone and usually did, John was fresh out of ideas on where to go with this one. He rubbed his hand down his jean-clad thigh and watched Darby stroke her fingers down her glass. She looked for a place to put it down, but he didn't have a coffee table, so she settled back, the glass still in her hands.

Despite all that had happened, he wanted her more than ever. That short time in the barn three months ago had been meant to assuage his desire for her. Instead, that desire had spiraled up to even greater heights. There wasn't a morning he didn't wake up imagining her soft moans, his palms itching to shape her breasts, pluck her taut nipples. And the taste of her. He swore he could still sense her there, on his tongue, sweet honey and saucy determination.

He cleared his suddenly tight throat. "So...who's watching the girls?"

He noticed the way she cleared her throat, as well. Had her mind been traveling down the same naughty road as his? "My mother. She, um, stopped by earlier for a visit and offered to stay when I told her I had to go out."

Her mother. Now there was a woman to put the fear of God into a guy. John shifted uncomfortably, thinking that what had happened with Dusty might be a piece of cake compared to what he'd probably suffer at Adelia Parker's hands. Adelia had raised her daughter all by herself when Darby's father had run out on them just before Darby was born. So it was understandable that she might be a little biased when it came to another man impregnating her daughter.

"Does she know?" he asked.

Darby shook her head. "I told her I was going to Jolie's."

"I meant about..."

"Oh!" Her cheeks flamed, making her that much prettier. "No. Word hasn't made it that far yet."

John sat forward, resting his forearms on his thighs. "From what I understand from Dusty, word isn't exactly out."

"How do you mean?"

"Tuck called him directly. Said he hadn't told another soul but that he felt Dusty should know."

"Kudos for Tuck," Darby whispered. "I wonder if it ever crossed his mind that I'd like to do the telling myself." Fire flashed in her eyes and John smiled. "What is it about men, anyway? Why do they feel they always have to protect women? That whole 'weaker sex' argument never cut it with me. I mean, Dusty isn't even technically my brother-in-law anymore. And anyway, the first place he should have gone with the information was my place. To talk to me. Not hunted you down and punched your lights out."

Well, that was certainly one way of putting it.

"He thought he was doing the right thing by you, Darby."

Her gaze slammed into his. And this time he was completely unable to read what she was thinking. Strictly because his libido kicked up and rendered him completely incapable of thinking anything at all.

Suddenly she was all heat and beauty and irresistible. She slowly got up and he made a sound deep in his throat as she moved the few feet necessary to sit next to him.

"I can't believe he did this," she said quietly, putting her hands on either side of his face, her gaze skimming his black eye. "I thought we'd advanced out of the Dark Ages."

John tensed, not quite knowing what to do when her mouth followed her gaze and she rested her lips against his injured eyelid. Fire, pure and undiluted, rushed straight to his groin.

"I'm tired of everyone doing what they think is the right thing for me," she whispered, her lips dropping to his cheek. "I think it's time for me to start doing what *I* think is right for me...."

Darby trailed her lips along the length of John's jaw, his skin like warm velvet. He smelled like soap. She flicked her tongue out, finding that he tasted like one hundred percent pure, needy male. And so very, very alive.

When Erick died, it was as if a fundamental part of her had died with him. The part that knew how to live. The part that threw caution to the wind and hungrily grabbed what she wanted. In its place grew fear. Fear of living. Fear of losing.

When Darby finally pressed her mouth to John's, she was filled with a longing so intense, so incredible, that she shuddered from her head to her toes. Oh, how she wanted this. Had wanted it ever since he'd last kissed her in the barn, in the aftermath of their lovemaking.

The truth was, she was tired of trying to do the

right thing. Fed up with townsfolk trying to help her and, instead, making a bigger mess for her to clean up. Angry that her ex-brother-in-law thought it his job to take care of her. From here on out, any trouble she got into would be hers and hers alone.

And oh, boy, was trouble with a capital *T* on her mind right now!

The expression on John's face was one of shock and confusion. Darby smiled slightly and then ran her tongue across his bottom lip, finally slipping it inside his mouth. The action seemed to trigger a switch and suddenly John's hands were in her hair, tugging her closer, his mouth crushing hers.

A sigh swept through Darby, taking her bones with it. She melted against him, her softness against his hardness. She'd be the first to admit that this was the last thing on her mind when she decided to come out here. But now that it was happening, she was glad it was. Something existed between her and John that no amount of rationalization could diminish. Not even the fact that she was pregnant could calm the clamoring of nerves for his touch, his kiss. Let the twins hate him. Despise her. She needed this. She needed John. Right here. Right now. Touching her. Kissing her. Making her feel like a woman. Not a mother. Not a wife. But a hungry, desirable female to his delectable male.

John groaned and increased the cadence of his kiss, his tongue sliding the length of hers, then retreating even as his hands sought and found her breasts beneath her shirt. Flames licked along Darby's skin, hardening her nipples, making her ache all over.

"Good God, woman," John ground out against her ear, holding her so close she could barely breathe. "Do you know what you're doing to me?"

Darby grasped his back tightly. "Oh, I don't know, but I think I'm trying to tempt you?" she whispered, moving just enough so their gazes could meet. "Seduce you?"

His pupils instantly took over the warm hazel of his eyes. "Is that what you're doing?"

She swallowed hard and tried for a smile, but it somehow didn't make it to her lips. Instead, it took up residence in her chest along with other burgeoning emotions. "I would be if you'd stop interrupting me."

With a groan, John roughly thrust a hand up into her hair and tugged her head back, gaining access to her throat. Shivers skittered down Darby's nerve endings, pooling in liquid heat between her thighs.

This couldn't possibly be even better than she remembered. But it was. Three months ago they'd had to contend with a blustery Ohio winter, most of their caresses made under cover of layers of clothing, their coming together as quick as possible. Darby had told herself at the time that that was why it had happened at all. It had all happened so fast, her hormones had burned so out of control, that had they taken their time, she would have backed out, stopped it from happening.

As she threaded her fingers through the strands of John's hair, reveling in the feel of his wet mouth nipping and kissing its way toward her breasts...well, she recognized that lie for what it was.

His lips nibbled at a hypersensitive nipple and she cried out.

With a sound deep in his throat, John picked her up and lay her across the soft leather of the couch, nudging open her knees with one of his before settling into the cradle of her thighs. The long ridge of his arousal pressed against her throbbing softness through her jeans. Heat arced through Darby, bringing her back up from the couch, her hands sliding down and over his hard rear. He felt so good. So hot.

John launched a fresh assault on her mouth, delving more deeply, breathing more heavily, and she responded with growing hunger. His fingers tunneled under her shirt again, not stopping until his hands cupped her breasts under her bra, teasing, plucking and caressing her flesh until she thought she would spontaneously combust.

"I want to see you," John whispered through her hair. "I want to see all of you."

She met his intense gaze and offered a tremulous smile. "What's stopping you?"

He began tugging at the buttons of her shirt. "This, for one."

She pushed at him gently until she'd gained enough room to stand. He reached for her and she stayed him with a hand. "Allow me," she said, standing beside the couch.

Feeling like a woman gone mad, she began slowly, deliberately undoing the remainder of buttons on her blouse, watching his eyes shift as he followed her movements, his eyes darkening further as each inch of flesh was revealed. Shrugging one shoulder, she allowed the material to drop halfway down her arm, then followed with the other, goose bumps peppering her skin. Not from the cold. Rather, from the gathering heat in John's eyes, on his face, the obvious restraint he used to stop himself as he lay on his side on the couch. As she shifted out of her bra, the air on her nipples made her shudder.

John tucked his fingers into the front catch of her jeans and hauled her forward, placing his hot wet mouth against her lower belly, then searing her skin with long laps of his tongue.

He gazed up at her, his expression serious, full of desire. "I can't believe you have our baby growing in there."

A different kind of heat surged through Darby's veins at his quiet wonder. She might have pulled away, but she suspected he wouldn't have allowed her the escape. Instead, she watched him close his eyes and slip the tip of his tongue into her belly button. He undid the button on her jeans, then slowly slid the zipper down, his decadent tongue following the opening metal until the elastic of her underpants stopped him. Or should have. Instead, he dipped his tongue into the waist of those, as well, and Darby's legs nearly gave out from under her.

She pulled away, suddenly urgent to strip all the way down. "Take off your clothes," she ordered.

He leaned back again, head propped up with his hand, watching as she shed her clogs and her jeans. When she slid her thumbs into her underpants, he stopped her. "No. Leave them. I want to do that."

Before she could blink, she was sitting on the

couch again. She knew a moment of self-con-sciousness as he knelt on the floor in front of her knees, his gaze raking her bare skin. Every nerve end-ing leaped, sizzled, longing for more than he was cur-rently giving her. She reached for him, but he caught her hands and held them at her sides briefly, before moving his fingers to the top of her underpants. Darby watched him, completely spellbound, as he slowly, torturously tugged them down, her springy dark curls emerging from the plain white cotton millimeter by millimeter. Finally all was revealed and she moved to cross her legs.

"Uh-uh. I want to see."

His hands splayed against her hips, holding her still.

Darby held her breath, waiting for what he would do next. But feeling his tongue burrowing through her curls, then finding the center of her womanhood was the last thing she would have expected. She threw her head back and moaned, her thighs automatically opening to allow him easier access.

"That's more like it," he murmured, but before she could respond, his tongue returned, laving circles around the tight pearl, around and around.

Darby's breath came in quick, ragged gasps and she found herself reaching for his head, torn between wanting to pull him away and needing to press him closer.

John grasped her hips and repositioned her so that she was in a semireclining position, her bottom even with the edge of the couch, her legs on either side of him. She automatically obeyed and wasn't disappointed when his mouth fastened over her again and began sucking.

The air around her drew in, then exploded outward in a mind-shattering burst. Waves of heat crashed and pounded through her as she grasped the cushion and cried out. But before she could explore the myriad wonderful, fascinating emotions the climax brought, John was filling her, his considerable length fitting tightly in her slick opening as her muscles contracted, his hands holding her hips still even as she instinctively strained against him.

Darby gasped, the decadent change in attention chasing her right over the edge again even as he brushed a thumb over her hooded flesh, drawing out her crisis.

Slowly, she drifted back to the couch and the mesmerizing man gazing at her. There lurked a dark intense shadow in his eyes. He moved his hips slightly, then slid back into her flesh, the sweet friction moving the heat in her abdomen up to her chest and back again. His strokes were controlled, measured...and made her want to make him lose control.

"John," she whispered harshly. "Please."

"Shh," he said, running a palm down her sweat-coated belly. "This time we do it my way."

Then he thrust hard and deep, filling her to overflowing, picking up his pace, driving into her flesh again and again and again, until the world shattered a second and then a third time, thrusting Darby into a world full of sensation, of desire, so unfamiliar that she was almost scared, but naughtily curious of it all the same. She clutched him, needing to feel him deeper, wanting him with an urgency that transcended anything she'd felt before.

Finally he tensed, his fingers biting into her hips, her name ripping from his throat as he drove all the way home and tilted her hips upward to allow him deeper access, taking her with him yet again.

## Chapter Seven

Darby lay on the couch in the cradle of John's arms, flesh on flesh, the spring night air on her skin chilly, but she was too drained, too sated to do much but vaguely wonder at it as John rained his fingertips up and down her bare back, eliciting a shiver.

She didn't quite know where they went from there. Didn't know if there was a "there" to work from. All she knew was that she'd needed this…closeness. This intimacy. And that John had given it to her. And right now that was all that mattered. She'd spent so much time over the past year looking at life from a wide angle. Trying so hard to find puzzle pieces she was beginning to suspect never existed or were gone forever, that somehow she'd forgotten how to just be. To enjoy each moment for all it was worth.

And John had brought that into focus with a few

wonderful caresses and passion enough for the both of them.

"Well," she said quietly, rubbing her nose against his hairless chest, "I'd say you've gotten over the surprise of my news quickly enough."

He remained silent, his fingers continuing their aimless movements on her back.

Darby cleared her throat and looked up at him. Mere moments ago, they'd been as one, sharing intimate secrets with each other's bodies. Now, as John stared at the ceiling, he couldn't have seemed farther away.

"John?" she whispered, trying to ignore the heat collecting in her belly yet again, despite his emotional distance.

John's hazel eyes shifted to her, and the somberness in them caused a shiver of a different sort to ripple over her skin. "I want you to promise me something, Darby."

So serious. Her throat tightened with the fear that he intended to propose to her again. A prospect that was part of that bigger picture she didn't want to have to deal with right then. She shifted to move away, but he only held her more tightly, his hands branding her bare skin.

His gaze moved from one of her eyes to the other, and she watched his Adam's apple bob in his throat. "No matter how it happened, where we go from here, I want you to promise me that you'll never make our baby feel like he or she was a mistake."

Darby's breath caught painfully. She lay her cheek back against his chest and closed her eyes, her arms around him, squeezing harder, listening to the cadence of his heartbeat beneath her ear. Never in a thousand years would she have imagined him saying anything of that nature, presenting her with that type of a request. "Of course I won't," she said quietly, wondering why he would think differently.

He gripped her arm, coaxing her to look at him again, his expression intense. "Promise me."

Darby swallowed hard, realizing how much this meant to him. "I promise," she whispered.

He seemed to measure her response, search her face for some sort of truth. Then he pulled her to him again, resting his chin on top of her head as she pondered the source of his request.

"Thank you."

Darby took a deep breath, then pressed a kiss to his warm skin and nestled closer.

She realized then that she knew precious little about John, about his upbringing, the obstacles, the inspirations that had turned him into the man he was. Yes, she knew he was from a large family. Everyone in Old Orchard was familiar with the Sparks family. It was hard to go anywhere without running into one of them. Especially now that the siblings had gone on and married, creating even more Sparkses. The only one left unmarried was John. And only now did that fact strike Darby as odd.

He was thirty years old to her twenty-eight. But where she'd already been married and had two children, she couldn't recall John ever having been serious with anyone.

"Erick was my best friend," he whispered so quietly Darby had to wonder whether he'd said the words or she'd imagined them.

She snuggled still closer. "Erick was my husband," she whispered back.

He shifted until he'd rolled her over, his eyes dark and weighty with feeling as he gazed at her. She gazed back, her own emotions running high. She could see the struggle raging within him. His need to be true to his best friend and his need for her at odds with the other.

She smiled softly and raised her hand to his face, wanting to tell him that it was okay. That what had begun three months ago hadn't been planned. Neither one of them had set out to betray anyone. Rather, they'd responded to a fundamental desire that still existed between them.

"It's important you know that," he said raggedly. "It's important to me that I remember that."

She nodded, speechless as he gently nudged her thighs open with his knee. He fit his arousal against flesh still slick and hot from their lovemaking. Her body strained upward as if to invite him inside. At the same time, she realized that she was responding to him as much on an emotional level as physical. And despite her fear of what opening her heart to him might lead to, she couldn't stop herself from doing so.

John drew his tongue slowly over her right nipple, then kissed his way up to her mouth.

He looked at her, the teasing back in his eyes. "By the way, I don't want you to think that I've forgotten."

She wriggled, trying to coax him into her hungry, waiting flesh. She restlessly licked her lips. "Forgotten what?"

"That I've yet to convince you to marry me."

Darby opened her mouth to protest and he entered her, sliding in to the hilt. Whatever response she might have made exited as a long moan.

The following day John looked at his watch for the third time in as many minutes. Never during his four years on the job had he wished for the time to pass. When he was on the job, he was on the job, no two ways about it. Outside concerns were kept outside. His mind was always firmly on what needed to be done.

Now, however, all he could think about was Darby, her sweet smile and her even sweeter flesh.

He dry-washed his face with his hands, then sat back in his chair, the squeak of the springs filling his empty office. God, but the woman was incredible. Sharp-tongued. Witty. And sexy as all get-out. He'd always known that, but after last night, knowing she was pregnant with his child, somehow made it all right to think of her in romantic terms. To envision her arching against him, his name on her lips. The images made him want to groan for completely different reasons.

He looked at his watch again. Not even lunchtime. He was going to go insane.

He sat up again and scanned his desktop. The ever-changing roster for the coming week begged for his attention. Old Mrs. Noonan's request for some uniformed men at next weekend's Easter-egg hunt all but leaped out at him. And the paperwork on the two fugitives in the holding cell waited for that call-back from the U.S. Marshal's office.

He frowned and flipped open the file. One Lyle Smythe, a twenty-nine-year-old Caucasian male, and Ted, his twenty-three-year-old brother, escaped from an Indiana high-security prison two months ago while tending to snow removal. Why both of them had been assigned to snow removal on the same day at the same time didn't make much sense. John rubbed the back of his neck and turned the page. The next one catalogued all the tattoos on the brothers' bodies. Quite a collection. Made them very easy to catch. A snake slithering up the neck of one was pretty hard to hide. He checked the information. Lyle was the snake guy.

Truth was, he didn't much like having those two stinking up his holding cell. That they were career criminals was evident. That they didn't like being in jail even more so.

If the U.S. Marshal Service was going to take long to pick the two up, he should consider separating them, perhaps moving the older one to the city police lockup just to be on the safe side.

John leaned forward, eyeballing Ed, who was chowing down on something or other for lunch. "Ed, did you get a chance to run that background check on the guys in the back?"

The older man sucked what looked like a piece of lettuce into his mouth and continued chewing. "Yeah. Ran it while you were out documenting that accident out on Route 108."

John sighed. "Where is it?"

"I put it on your desk."

John rifled through the papers littering the top. No printout.

"Oh, wait a minute." Ed got up from the counter, his sandwich in one hand, papers in the other. "I have them here." He slapped the printouts down on top of the desk, smearing mayonnaise all over the top page. "Sorry," he said, swiping at the mess with a napkin.

John waved him away. "I got it. Go back to the front before I catch you trying to lick it off."

Ed grinned and took another bite of his sandwich. "You sure you don't want some of this?"

"No, I think I'll pass," John said, envisioning the desk sergeant breaking off a piece of the slobbered-on sandwich and handing it to him.

Ed shrugged, then returned to the front.

Shaking his head at the tall, skinny man who ate enough to put a horse to shame but never gained a pound, John wiped off the mayo with a paper towel he took from a roll in a desk drawer. Then, tossing the towel into the wastebasket, he leaned back in his chair again and took the papers with him. His eyebrows rose as he read down the long list of convictions. Robbery. Armed robbery. Forgery. Breaking and entering. Resisting arrest. Car theft. Name any crime short of assault and murder, these two had done it.

He was reaching for the sheet outlining the unsolved felonies in the county, then for the log of unsolved felonies statewide, when the phone rang. He set the papers down and picked up the receiver on the third ring.

"Sparks here."

"Well, hello there, Sheriff. Which uniform are you wearing today? The gray-and-black one or the black-and-gray one?" Darby's voice filtered across the line.

"My mother always said there's something about a guy in uniform."

John snapped upright so fast the springs in the chair nearly catapulted him across the desk. He smoothed his tie as if she could see him through the telephone line. "I think she was talking about the military," he managed, although his pulse had kicked up.

Her answering laugh made him grin. She had the kind of infectious laugh that could make a funeral wake seem like an occasion to celebrate. Movement in the other room caught his attention. He looked up to find Ed craning his neck to ferret out whom he was talking to.

John cleared his throat and giveaway expression. "Something I can do for you?"

"Oh, I don't know. It all depends on how long you can get away from the office."

John nearly choked. "You're one dangerous woman, do you know that?"

"Hmm, I've never thought about it before, but I think I may be a bit dangerous. In fact, maybe you should pull me in off the streets. I've never worn handcuffs before."

The thought of handcuffs and a naughtily naked Darby nearly sent John into cardiac arrest.

There was a muffled sound, then he heard Darby say, "Erin, I don't think Spot wants to wear makeup."

John hiked a brow.

"Anyway," she said, talking to him again, "I just called, you know, to see how you're doing."

"I'm fine," he said. "And you?"

"More than fine."

He swiveled his chair away from Ed and grinned again. "Yeah, me, too."

"I was talking about your eye."

"Oh." He lifted a hand and probed the area in question. The pain had passed, but it would take a good week for the bruise to fade to nothing. "I think I'll live."

"If you didn't, it would probably be the first documented case of a man perishing from a black eye."

"Very funny."

Her laugh made heat snake through his body. "Look, John, I also called to ask what you're doing for dinner tonight."

"I thought I'd nuke the frozen chicken nuggets I have in the freezer, you know, before they go bad. Can you come up with something to top that?"

"How's lasagna sound?"

"Better than frozen chicken nuggets." He knew a moment of hesitation as memories of the other night drifted through his mind. His grin vanished. "Are you sure the twins want me there?"

"I'm sure I want you here," she said quietly. "There's something I think we need to talk about."

This was it. She was going to say yes to his proposal.

John's heart banged against his ribs so hard he could almost see it. "Oh."

"Is that a yes?"

"No."

"No?"

"I mean yes."

He imagined her thousand-watt smile. "Good. I'll see you around six, then?"

"Yes. Wearing full body armor."

"Ha ha."

John slowly replaced the receiver. Dear Lord, he was going to be a married man.


"I don't like 'sagna."

Darby blew out a long, patient breath as she considered Erin's stubborn face. She glanced at Lindy, standing slightly behind her sister and to the side, then back again. "Don't be silly. Lasagna is one of your favorites."

"Well, I decided I don't like it anymore."

*O-okay,* Darby thought.

Her first mistake had been telling Erin and Lindy their uncle Sparky was coming over for dinner. Constantly underfoot, the twins with their sulky expressions found ways to trip her up at every turn. From placing an in-line skate in her path to spilling watercolor paint all over the kitchen table, they seemed to have declared some sort of war on her. A war she was afraid she was losing.

"Tell you what," she said with dwindling patience. "If, when we sit down to eat in a little while, you no longer want lasagna, I'll make you something else, okay?"

"What?"

"I don't know," Darby said, shrugging. "Cereal."

"But that's breakfast food."

"It's still food."

Erin made an unhappy face and turned around, no doubt intending to regroup and plan her next attack. Darby met Lindy's eyes, wondering what was going on in her other daughter's head. She'd been awfully quiet lately. Which was a good thing, she supposed, considering how much talking Erin had been doing.

Darby smiled. "Would you like to help me set the table, Lin?"

The six-year-old blinked, then headed for the side door. "I think I forgot to feed Billy his dinner."

Darby blew her bangs from out of her eyes, wondering where the two little cherubs from the other day had gone and just what she had to do to get them back. Something that didn't include indulging their new, hostile feelings for John.

She remembered his comment about wearing full body armor for dinner. She hoped he hadn't been joking.

Darby glanced at the clock, disappointed to find that she wouldn't have time to change into the pink dress she'd laid out on her bed earlier. She took a moment to tuck a few stray strands of hair back into her French braid, which was all the time she could spare for her appearance as she closed the foil around the fresh garlic bread and put the loaf in next to the lasagna in the oven.

"Hello."

Darby's every nerve ending hummed to life at the sound of John's quiet voice directly behind her. She glanced to where Lindy must have left the door open on her way outside, then turned to face the man who had occupied so much of her thoughts all day long.

"Hello, yourself," she said.

She allowed her gaze to leisurely rake him from the tip of his scuffed cowboy boots, up his faded jeans, over his soft-purple chambray shirt, then up to where his hair was still slightly wet from a shower.

She breathed in the tangy scent of soap and shaving cream.

He looked good. Damn good. And made her feel even better just standing there looking at him.

Something hit the back of her legs, jarring her from her thoughts and nearly off her feet. Stifling a vocal exclamation, she turned to find Erin had just plowed into her with one of the four chairs. She caught it with both hands. "Where do you think you're going with that?"

"Lindy needs help with Billy."

Darby refused to relinquish her hold even as her daughter pushed. She realized Erin was trying to get rid of the chair John was to use. "And you need the chair to do that?"

"The fence is high."

"The fence has a gate, which you know how to open."

Erin rolled her eyes and finally let go of the chair, although she was none too happy about it. "I'm going outside."

"Good," Darby said, then bit her tongue.

Erin glared at John and the flowers in his hands, then stomped toward the door.

The kitchen loomed large and silent for a full minute after she slammed the door.

Darby rubbed her forehead and gave a small laugh. "Sorry about that. I still haven't figured out what's going on."

John grimaced, watching through the open door as Erin trudged toward the barn. "I think I know."

Darby glanced at him.

"They don't want me to marry you."

She smiled at him even though her heart had leaped to her throat. "Well, then, we don't have anything to worry about there, do we? Because I'm not going to marry you."

John blinked. "I don't get it. Isn't that why you called me out here?"

"Is that why you came?"

"Do you always have to answer a question with a question?"

She chuckled, feeling the tension of the past hour melt away. God, it felt good to laugh.

John said something under his breath, then held out the bouquet of fresh daisies mixed with wildflowers. "These are for you." A shadow of something familiar yet unfamiliar entered his eyes. He slid a glance toward the door, then backed Darby out of the line of the girls' vision and up against the counter where he kissed her. Soundly. His mouth a reminder of the passion they had experienced last night.

Darby blindly put the flowers on the counter behind her and curved her arms around him, sliding her palms over his firm behind. Only when her knees threatened to give out from under her did he pull away and grin, running his index finger under his lips. "How can you say no to something I haven't asked yet?"

She cleared her throat, feeling as internally in disarray as she was physically. "John…"

She was afraid he was going to drop to one knee again and braced herself. Instead, he grasped her waist and hoisted her onto the countertop, her jean-clad behind settling right in the middle of the flower stems. She opened her mouth to protest, but he lay a finger over her lips, then cupped her face with both hands. He looked at her for a long moment and then kissed her, taking her breath away. ''Marry me, Darby.''

Was it her, or was it a little more difficult to say no today? ''No.''

His grimace was all too endearing.

''I need to know, John, is there, um, any three-strike rule here?'' She smiled, grabbing his hands when he would have stepped away. ''Sorry, bad joke.''

He stared at her as if trying to figure her out. ''So why did you invite me over here tonight?''

Now there was a question.

''It can't have been just to feed me.''

Darby glanced at the clock. ''Speaking of feeding, I'd better take the lasagna out or we'll all be eating cereal tonight.''

''Cereal?''

John stepped back and allowed her to slide off the counter to stand on the floor. ''Long story,'' she said.

So how did one go about broaching a subject of this delicate matter, anyway? she wondered.

''Why do I get the feeling you're avoiding my question?'' John asked as she grabbed a pair of oven mitts and emptied the oven of its steaming contents.

She smiled at him over her shoulder. ''Maybe because I am?''

''Trust me, after the past few days, I don't think there's anything you could say that could shock me.''

She put the mitts down on the counter. ''You want to bet?''

He chuckled.

"I want you to help me tell the girls that they're going to have a little sister or brother in six months."

John looked as if someone had just hit him upside the head with a two-by-four. "Then there's that."

Dinner was an unqualified disaster. John sported no fewer than three food groups on the front of his shirt, felt a tremendous thirst for water because one of the twins had emptied nearly the entire contents of a salt-shaker on his food while he was talking to the other one, and to top it off, Spot had declared open season on his pant leg, batting and clawing as if she wanted him to do something he wasn't. If he didn't know better, he'd think the cat was in cahoots with the girls.

John leaned over to whisper something to Darby, who sat in the armchair next to him in the living room, the twins sitting stiffly on the couch opposite them. "Tell me, are you going to make a habit out of this shocking-me stuff?"

Darby's smile was full of brightness and light when all he felt like doing was crawling out of the house on all fours. "Not having a change of heart, are you?"

"Never."

"Then from here on out it'll be my mission in life to present you with at least one shocking development a day."

"Damn."

Erin spoke up. "Mama, he said a cussword." She started to get up from the couch.

Darby held up her hand. "Whoa there a minute. Where do you think you're going?"

"To get the soap."

John's brows hiked and he looked at Darby. It was all too obvious that she was stifling a laugh.

"That won't be necessary, sweetie. It was just a little slip. Nothing that warrants having his mouth washed out."

Erin looked as if it was a capital offense and she was willing to try all the same.

"You're not getting married, are you?"

John blinked at Lindy, who for the most part had stayed quiet throughout dinner. Her lips were pink from where she'd eaten strawberry breakfast cereal, instead of lasagna. But it was the pain in her soft brown eyes that hit John like a punch to the gut.

"No, honey, John and I aren't getting married."

John sat forward, resting his forearms against his knees. "That's not exactly decided yet," he corrected. "You see, I still want to marry your mother. And I don't intend to take the no she's been giving me for an answer."

Dead silence.

John cleared his throat. "Tell me, Erin and Lindy, would it bother you if your mom and I did get married?"

Both girls immediately started nodding.

"Why?"

The girls looked at each other for a long moment, but said nothing.

Darby raised her brows at him and he shrugged helplessly, praying she'd rescue him.

She did. But didn't continue on the marriage topic.

"But that's not what I...what we want to talk to you about, Erin, Lindy," she said quietly, looking at each twin in turn. "You see, there are going to be some changes around here in the coming months, and I...we think it's only fair that you learn about them from us, instead of someone else.''

Erin folded her arms stubbornly across her chest, while Lindy sank a little more deeply into the cushions.

''What John and I want to say—''

''I already know,'' Erin said.

Darby leaned back. ''I see. And what do you think you know, Erin?''

''That you're going to have a stupid baby.''

John nearly fell out of his chair.

Yep, it was very clear they did already know.

## Chapter Eight

The girls knew? John thought. But how? From whom? And how much did they know?

"I see," Darby said, speaking when he could not. "And you understand that John is going to be the father of that baby?"

Erin looked about ready to vibrate from the couch she was so upset. "I know that he got you pregnant. That he did something bad to you and now you're going to get fat, and be grumpy, and throw up all the time."

"Erin!" Darby admonished. "Where did you hear all this?"

"From Joshua McCreary up the road."

Darby looked at John, but he'd long since passed the point of response. "Joshua's mother just had a baby," she explained to him.

"Uh, oh," he managed, and cringed.

Had it really been all that long since he'd been a kid? With a sinking sensation, he realized it had. Ever since the twins were born, he'd been the fun uncle. The one that got to play with them and didn't have to discipline them. Who told them neat jokes and laughed at all of theirs. Who knew just where to tickle them to get the biggest reaction. But he had no idea what to say to them now, when they needed answers.

Maybe that was because he was a little short on answers himself just now.

"Joshua was, um, right, in some respects." Darby cleared her throat. "But way off base on others. What happened between John and me…it wasn't bad, Erin. And I don't want you ever to think that it was."

She paused and John picked up the gauntlet. "You guys and I have always been pals, haven't we, Erin? Lindy?"

Both girls stared at their laps.

"I'd like to continue that relationship," he went on doggedly. "Just because your mom and I are having a baby doesn't mean your mom is going to love you less. Or that I won't love you anymore."

"You don't love us," Erin said.

Darby's heart sank as she watched John wince from each of the jabs her daughter delivered. She started to say something, but he held his hand up to stop her. "Let me," he said quietly.

She mentally groaned, knowing that he'd seen only the tip of the iceberg and hoped he was ready for whatever else the twins decided to reward him with.

She was surprised, however, when he got up from

the chair and moved around the coffee table to stand in front of the girls. "Do you mind if I sit here?"

Neither of them said anything, but they did inch over, although not enough for him to sit. So John plucked them both up, one in each arm, sat down, then resettled them so they sat on either side of him.

Darby fought a smile at the girls' wide-eyed expressions now that something, or rather someone, blocked their conspiratorial exchange of glances.

"Now which one of you said I didn't love you?" John asked, tapping a finger against his lips as he looked at first one twin, then the other. "Ah. I remember. It was Erin." He narrowed his gaze on the little girl, twisting his lips in mock thought. Erin fidgeted. "Is that what you really think? That I don't love you?"

All the starch seemed to drain from Erin as she shrugged. "Why should you love us? We're not your kids."

"No, you're right. We're not blood-related," he agreed. "But if there were two little girls I could choose to be my daughters in the whole wide world, you know who I'd pick?"

"Us?" Lindy asked from the other side.

John smiled at her, taking her tiny hand in his large one and giving a squeeze. "That's right. You. And Erin." He took the other twin's hand, then drew both hands on top of his lap.

Darby felt like all twenty digits encircled her heart, and it suddenly became difficult to breathe.

"What about the new baby?" Erin asked.

John met Darby's gaze and she couldn't help feeling sorry for him—she could see the spark of panic in his eyes. "I don't know. What about the new baby, Mommy?" he asked.

Darby's voice caught. She cleared her throat and said, "The new baby will just be one more very special little person to love."

"But what if there isn't enough love?" Lindy asked.

"No such thing," John said, comically shaking his head. "There's always enough love." He patted the couch on the other side of Erin. "Why don't you come over here and help explain, Mom?"

Darby wasn't sure her knees would allow her to move, but she made an effort and managed to edge around the coffee table. She sat down on the couch and John lifted Lindy, putting both twins between them, his arm resting on the back of the couch.

"I think an analogy is in order here. A comparison," she said. "You remember when Curly the Piglet was left at our door?"

The twins nodded.

"Well, we didn't say, 'Hmm, I wonder if we have enough love for this new animal who needs a home and someone to look after him.' We just saw him and the love appeared."

"Like magic," Lindy said.

Darby kissed the top of her head, eyeing John over the top. "Yes, sweet pea, just like magic."

John's fingers sought and found Darby's shoulder. She relaxed into his touch, bone-deep gratitude saturating her muscles, desire sizzling along her nerve endings. Erin caught John's movement and made a face.

"Okay," the six-year-old said, all energy and spice again. "We all love each other. But that still doesn't mean you two can get married."

"Why not?" John asked.

"Because Lindy and I don't want you to, that's why."

Erin scooted from the couch, then reached out for her sister's hand. "Come on, Lin. We've got to go get ready for bed."

Darby gave John a warning glance. The twins had gone as far as they were going to go for one night, and forcing the issue would only jeopardize any ground gained. "I'll be in in a minute to read your bedtime story," she said as they disappeared up the stairs.

John collapsed against the couch cushions, rubbing a finger and thumb over his closed eyes. "I feel like I just went ten rounds with Ali."

She leaned over, brushing his lips with hers. His eyes opened. "It looks like you did, too."

She got up from the couch. "I'll only be a little while. Wait for me?"

He seemed to consider that. "Depends on what you had in mind."

She smiled. "Unfortunately, not what you think."

"Then I think I'll go."

She laughed. "Why don't you go make us some coffee while I go introduce two munchkins to the sandman?"

* * *

John hadn't been lying. One of the most difficult challenges he'd ever had to face was those two girls gazing at him implacably with questions he didn't know the answers to. He sank onto a kitchen chair as the coffee brewed, wondering how his own parents had done it. Of course he remembered there being countless because-I-said-so's and countless times his father just threw his hands up in the air and left the room.

John leaned forward and absently rubbed the back of his neck, afraid he was getting but a glimpse of what life would be like from here on out. How complicated it would become, where once it had been simple.

Then there was the small fact that Darby wanted to talk to him, apparently determined to make good on her threat to keep surprising him.

He got up and went on the hunt for coffee mugs, finding a couple in the dishwasher. He'd thought that telling the twins about the baby had been solely what she'd been after. And since, apparently, her asking him to stay didn't have anything to do with repeating last night...

God, last night. How long ago it seemed. Yet how immediate, given the reaction of his body. Whenever he and Darby were in close proximity, he felt his pulse rate spike, his palms grow damp and a subtle sizzling awareness of her flow through his body. But last night...wow.

He closed his eyes and reminded himself that what she had to say had nothing to do with that.

"Are you okay?"

John tensed at the sound of her voice right behind him. He turned. "Marry me, Darby," he said.

She smiled, but averted her gaze. "No."

Was it him, or did it take her a little longer to say no this time?

"That's not why I asked you to stay." Her lips twisted. Her full, luscious lips that John longed to kiss now that the twins weren't underfoot. "Then again, maybe it is."

John lifted a hand to his head. "Boy, Darby, if you want me to follow, you're going to have to be a little clearer than that."

She stepped to the counter next to him, the clean smell of her filling his senses. She continued what he had begun and poured the coffee, then handed him a cup. "What I mean is, well, I've been doing some thinking."

"When?" he asked, because over the past couple of hours he hadn't been able to keep a sane thought in his head.

"Now. Earlier." She sat down at the table and he did likewise, his gaze sliding down her slender neck to where the V of her shirt played peek-a-boo with her sweet flesh. He focused in on her face and found her smiling. "You were great with the girls, by the way." She pushed her thick dark hair back behind her ears and held it there, giving him an unobstructed view of her neck and her thrumming pulse. "I'm coming to think that you're a natural. I mean, I always knew you were good with the girls. Especially after...."

Erick died. She didn't have to say it. The unsaid words hung between them, anyway.

Following long moments of silence, Darby sighed. "Well, talk about a conversation stopper."

John nodded, his fingers wrapped tightly around his coffee cup. "I know this isn't easy for you, Darby. None of it has been." He sat back. "Hell, it hasn't been easy for any of us."

Her warm green eyes were fixed on him.

He couldn't help a small smile. "Erick's girl. That's what you were. The minute you two started going out, I made myself repeat that a million times, just to drill it into my head. You were my best friend Erick's girl. Which meant you were off-limits to me."

Her gaze drifted to her coffee.

"And if he hadn't died eleven months ago, you'd still be Erick's girl." He rubbed his face, then sighed, staring at the wedding band still on her ring finger. "What am I talking about? You're still Erick's girl. It doesn't matter if he's here or if he's gone. You'll always belong to him, won't you? That's why you keep saying no to me."

Darby looked, for a minute, as if she had difficulty breathing. "Love doesn't die with death, John. If that makes any sense."

He nodded. Her words made perfect sense. His own feelings for his best friend would never die.

"But that isn't why I can't marry you."

"Can't."

She blinked at him. "What?"

"You said can't. Not won't. Or shouldn't."

She waved her hand. "Forget my word usage for

a minute, okay?'' She took a long sip of coffee, suddenly looking troubled. ''Let me ask you something, John.''

He nodded. ''Anything.''

''Did you ever doubt Erick's love for you? You know, as a friend?''

John widened his eyes. What kind of question was that? ''Never. Not once.''

The smile she gave him was almost sad. ''Yes, well, you're lucky, then. Because it was something I wondered about almost every day.''

John sat back, stunned. ''Was it something he said? Did?''

She shook her head. ''No, no. Nothing like that. It was…it was because we had to get married that made me wonder.'' She squinted at him. ''Are you getting where I'm coming from?''

He was. All too clearly. And he didn't like the picture she painted. ''Erick loved you more than anything in this world, Darby. You had to know that.''

Saying the words ignited a dull ache in John's gut. Simply because it was strange to be sitting here with the woman he wanted to sleep with, the woman who was pregnant with his child, and tell her that her late husband loved her.

''I did know it. Sometimes.''

''Sometimes.''

John got the feeling that Erick wouldn't be happy at all to hear his wife say this.

''That's why…that's why I can't marry you, John. Somewhere in my mind, I'd always wonder, you know? Did he marry me just because I was pregnant? Or because he…'' Her words drifted off.

*Or because he loves me?*

John got up abruptly from the table.

''John?'' She reached out and touched his arm. He looked down at her. At her beautiful face. The question in her eyes. The sexy curve of her lips.

''I've got to go.''

''But I still haven't said what I meant to.''

John brushed his knuckles along the curve of her cheek. ''I think enough has been said for one night, don't you?''

He took his denim jacket from the coat tree in the corner and shrugged into it, watching her stare at her coffee. Just when he thought he had everything straight, a different layer was revealed, another dimension, making him wonder if he'd ever figure it out. And it scared the hell out of him.

''Thank you,'' he said, gripping the doorknob.

She looked at him. ''For what?''

He shrugged. For what, indeed? For making him feel like a heel for hurting her and straining her relationship with her kids? ''For, um, dinner.''

She smiled. ''Anytime.''

Darby exchanged her coffee for a cup of warm milk, then curled up on the couch, an Ohio State Buckeyes stadium blanket warding off the chill of the spring night. She'd given up on the remote, and the television flicked silent images across the screen because she'd muted the sound. Not even her work could hold her attention. Photographs were strewn across the coffee table in front of her. She'd intended to choose from the various shots she'd taken of rural Old Orchard for framing, but realized after the third go-round that she wasn't seeing the pictures at all.

She propped her head in her hand. What had she been thinking, telling John what she had? The truth was she hadn't been thinking. Rather, on some fundamental level she'd felt the need to talk to him about Erick, about her marriage to her late husband, and her mouth automatically followed.

It was important that he know the reason, the real reason, she couldn't marry him.

She reached out and plucked up the ring she'd meant to return to him off the table and clicked open the box. The gold was warm on her index finger as she worried it around and around, contrasting it against her platinum wedding band. On those days when she knew with her entire being that Erick loved her for her, not just because she was the mother of his children, life had been good. Very good. And when he'd died…well, she'd never expected to love again. Not in the same intense way that left her in a mess of hormones and drowning in a sea of insecurity. Yet here she was wondering what John was doing right now, feeling his presence in the house as surely as if he was still there. And she'd known the moment that had happened, the moment he'd stolen a piece of her heart. Well, maybe she didn't know the exact moment that had happened, but she did know when she grew aware of his holding such a key part of her in his hands: When she'd watched him with the girls earlier. When he'd patted the sofa and asked her to come sit with them as if they were a family, and more. She'd known in that moment that he'd make a wonderful husband. And a terrific father.

She slid the ring back into the box. No, she couldn't marry him. But she did want him to play an important role not only in their baby's life, but also in the twins'. And she'd hoped to do that with a proposal of her own until he'd practically run from her and what she'd been trying to say to him.

She put the box down on top of the pictures and glanced at the cordless phone on the table next to her. No, her words were better said in person. But right now she didn't have that option. And they were words that needed to be said.


John shut the door behind him, grabbed a beer out of the refrigerator, popped the top and walked into the living room. Tossing his jacket onto the back of the recliner, he tipped the bottle and drank from it until he had to come up for air.

He ran the back of his hand across his mouth and cursed a blue streak. What was it about Darby Parker Conrad that made him want to run out of the trailer and shout at the top of his lungs? He felt ready to burst, the emotions in him accumulating, mutating, taking over his body and mind until he didn't recognize himself. Oh, he was still the sheriff of Old Orchard County. That hadn't changed. But even standing there in the trailer, a place that had served just fine as his home for the past six years, made him feel like a foreigner, as if he no longer belonged there and knew it. Whereas he would have automatically taken a seat in the recliner and clicked on the television to see if some game or other was playing, now he didn't quite know where to sit.

Damn, but the woman had evicted him from his own skin. And she didn't have one clue how he really felt about her.

Of course he was a little fuzzy on that detail himself, so he couldn't really blame her.

He caught himself staring at the leather sofa, remembering her pale skin and dark hair against it, her back arched in passion, her nipples pert, delectable peaks....

He cursed again, then dropped into the recliner and kicked off his boots. The place was quiet. Too quiet. Yet he didn't want to turn on the TV or the radio. He merely sat there staring at the opposite wall, replaying the words she'd said earlier in his mind.

*I never knew if Erick loved me for me, or because I was the mother of his children.*

Was she insane? Didn't she know that a million men would be standing in line if they thought they stood a fraction of a chance with her? Of course Erick had loved her. To pieces. What wasn't there to love? She was beautiful. Sexy. Down-to-earth. The most courageous woman he'd ever known.

So what was he saying? That he loved Darby?

He scratched his brow and took another swig of beer, the barley drink bitter on his tongue.

He honestly didn't know. He desired her. Hell, physically he wanted her beyond reason.

What he did know was that she deserved to be

loved. Loved the way Erick had loved her. Deserved to love the way she had loved Erick.

He grimaced, realizing that was where his thoughts had been leading him all along. To the fear that if he could get Darby to love him, she'd never do so the way she'd loved Erick. Somewhere in the back of her mind she'd always be thinking of the man she'd lost. The man who had been taken from her. The father of her girls. He could never hope to take Erick's place. Was surprised that he even wanted to.

No, not surprised. He'd always envied, in a way, what Erick had. Despite his stance on marriage, he'd often found himself looking at his best friend, wondering at the grin on his face, the wife he had at home, the kids who loved him, the house that had everything a home should.

And if that wasn't enough, Erick had gotten to make love to Darby every night....

John pushed himself out of the recliner, then went out to the sink and poured the remainder of the beer down the drain. Sitting around here doing nothing but thinking certainly wasn't getting him anywhere. Maybe he should head to the office, see what was going on and check in on their temporary prisoners. He'd just gone into the bathroom, switched on the shower and was stripping off his clothes when he heard the phone ring. Someone from the office? was his first thought. He switched off the water and, clad in only his jeans, stepped into the bedroom to pick up the extension there.

"Hi," Darby's voice filtered over the line.

A knot tightened in John's stomach. "Hi."

A hesitation. In fact, her greeting had sounded a little reluctant, as if she wanted to say something, but wasn't sure how to go about saying it.

"I'm not interrupting anything, am I?" she asked quietly.

"No." John scratched his head, then ruffled his hair. "I was just thinking about heading downtown."

"Something happen?"

"No. Just thought I'd check on things, that's all." *And get out of this trailer before I go crazy thinking about you. About being with you. Making love to you until you cry out my name, instead of Erick's.*

"The twins?" he asked.

"Fast asleep."

"That's good."

"Yeah."

He winced at the mundanity of their conversation, then glanced at the clock to find it was after eleven. "Is there something in particular you wanted?"

He hated that he sounded abrupt, but just hearing her voice made him aroused, and if he didn't end the call but quick he was afraid he'd say something he'd regret. Like ask her if he could come back over.

"Yes, there is something I wanted," she said, some mettle back in her voice. "I didn't get a chance earlier. Anyway, I have a proposal of my own I'd like to make."

John sat down on the bed and switched the receiver to the other ear.

"Maybe not so much a proposal, really. Maybe it's more of a compromise."

"Go on."

She took a deep breath, her soft sigh drifting over the line and making him want her even more. "Move in here with me and the twins."

John felt as if someone had just dumped a bucket of ice water on his head. "What?"

"Temporarily. I'll fix up the guest room. You can stay as long or as little as you'd like. Not as husband and wife, you understand, but as...parents to be. That way you can be involved in the pregnancy. The birth, even. You know, if you want..."

Seldom were the times he'd heard Darby babble. And she was definitely babbling. That he was the cause of it made something interesting ignite in his chest.

"So what do you say?"

## Chapter Nine

On the other end of the phone line, Darby mashed her eyes shut, waiting for John's response.

When she'd initially considered making the proposal, she'd had no idea how it would actually sound coming out of her mouth. She decided she'd come off like an idiot. A woman who didn't know what she wanted except for everything and everyone to be happy.

"What will the town say?" John asked.

"What?" She stared at the receiver. Then she caught the teasing in his voice and relaxed against the cushions, tension oozing out of her. "They'll probably think we're having wild-monkey sex in every corner of the house."

"And will we?"

Darby's heart skipped a beat and she licked suddenly dry lips. "Um, no, John. If you agree to this, I'll have to insist you stay in the guest room. The girls…well, they're already confused enough." To say nothing of her own emotional condition. She knew she could connect some of her moodiness to her pregnancy, but not all of it.

"There's always the barn," John suggested.

She smiled as her hand made absent circles around her stomach. Was it her, or did she feel a slight *poof?* Was her, their, baby already beginning to let herself be known? "Didn't that get us into enough trouble the last time?"

"Well, since we're already in as deep as we can get…"

Were they? Darby wasn't convinced. She was beginning to fear that where they stood now was just the start of a long, emotional roller-coaster ride she wasn't sure she was up to.

But John did deserve to be involved in as much of the birthing process as possible. She wanted their baby to bond with him. Know him the way she did. Love him. To know that he returned that love. Just the way her mother's love for her had always been unfaltering.

And if John's staying here, getting a real taste of what life at the farm was like also served to scare him but good, well, that was in her best interests, too.

"So when do we do this?" John asked, clearing his throat.

"Um, I think I should tell the girls first." And her mother, and her brother-in-law, and Jolie…

"Why don't we do it together?"

Gratitude filled in her chest. "I'd like that." Even if she would be on her own in everything else, she'd welcome his support with the twins. In some ways, the girls seemed to respond better to him than her. Familiarity dictated that they knew what buttons to push to get the response they wanted from her. John, however, was an unknown quantity. And as such had a much better chance of success.

"Let's say tomorrow night?"

He was silent.

"John?" She hated the plaintive sound of her voice, but was afraid he was having second thoughts. She didn't realize how invested she was in the hope that his staying there would scare him off the topic of marriage until she thought he might not go with her plan.

"I'm here," he said, then fell silent again. "Tell me, Darby," he said at last. "What are my chances of getting you to agree to go the whole nine yards?"

"Marriage?" Her gaze locked onto the ring box on the table in front of her. "Oh, about zero to none."

"Remember you said that." She heard the grin in his voice. "See you tomorrow at six."

"Okay," she said softly, but realized he hadn't heard her. He'd already hung up.

She put the cordless back down on the table next to her, wondering at the slight trembling of her hand. In less than twenty-four hours John would be here, in the house, not as a guest, but as a part of it. No matter how temporary the arrangement, Darby found that her body sang. And that the slightest bit of fear began to blossom in her stomach, fear that John would never give up trying to get her to marry him.

She stared at the wedding band she still wore. For some reason she was surprised to still find it there. A reaction that didn't make any sense because she didn't remember taking it off. It just suddenly seemed... inappropriate to be wearing it now.

For long minutes she sat still, merely staring at the circle of metal and all it had once signified. She'd always wondered when would be the right time to remove her wedding ring. She twisted the band around her finger, then halfway removed it before sliding it home again. She'd assumed she'd know when the right time was.

Swallowing hard, she closed her eyes and completely removed the ring. She waited for guilt to assault her. A sense of wrongness. Instead, she felt a rightness so complete, so overwhelming, that it nearly took her breath away. She closed her fingers around the warm metal. One word echoed through her mind. "Goodbye." And she knew she wasn't only saying a final farewell to her husband, but to life as she'd known it before.

Three days later Darby set the coffeemaker to brew, then snuggled more deeply into her terry-cloth robe, trying to ward off the spring-morning chill. She hadn't slept very well last night. Hadn't slept well for the past two nights, if she was being honest. Ever since John had easily taken up residence in the guest room down the hall from her room.

She glanced out the back window, at the crisp frost

still on the ground and the strong sun just breaking the horizon. She didn't know how, but already it seemed they'd settled into a routine. Every morning she got up first, put on the coffee, started breakfast, got the twins up and ready to go to school, then John stumbled downstairs in his black uniform pants, his gray shirt left open to reveal the rippling muscles of his abdomen. And every morning she watched him, longing for something she had forbidden either of them to have, but thought about every moment of every night, robbing her of much-needed sleep.

It would help if she knew he felt the same. But she suspected that when they parted ways every night, saying an awkward good-night in the upstairs hall, he didn't give her a second thought. If the soft snoring she'd heard the first night when she'd padded barefoot to stand outside his door was any indication, he dropped into bed and was dead to the world until the following morning.

While she lay, a trembling pile of needy hormones, three doors up.

Of course, it couldn't be easy for him having a houseful of people when he was used to just having himself to contend with. The twins even on a good day could be a handful. And the past three days had definitely not been good days. They had not been pleased with Uncle Sparky's taking up residence in their house. The first night, she'd heard one or the other of them, possibly both, get up no fewer than three times to make sure the adults in the house were in their own beds. She smiled now, wondering just who was supposed to be the parent, and who the children. They took great relish in giving John a hard time at every turn. Asking him to read them a book, then changing the reading material halfway through, so that by the time the twins finally dropped off to sleep, he'd read them a good chunk of at least three of their thickest offerings.

She eyed the brewing coffee longingly, then sighed when she found it wasn't even halfway ready. Instead, she opened the cellar door, switched on the light and descended the stairs. Some homemade marmalade might be nice on this morning's toast.

Okay, she admitted to herself, maybe she liked having a man around the house again. So far, John had proved inexhaustible in seeing to chores that had gone undone for months. The upstairs bathroom door that stuck. The cracked front basement window. The drip under the kitchen sink that she'd been using a bucket to catch for the past five months. And the tasks were made doubly difficult by the presence of two would-be helpers who seemed hell-bent on making his life miserable.

Upstairs she heard the sound of scuffling feet and frowned. She'd woken the girls, but it usually took them a good three wake-up calls before they finally got up. She eyed the marmalade and wondered what they were up to now.

John tried to hold on to the dream. Wispy, sexy images of Darby writhing beneath him, her back arched, her mouth swollen from his kisses, her fingers in his hair. But the more he tried to hold on, the more the visions slipped away. Except for the hair part. He grinned and settled more deeply into the pillows, allowing himself the luxury of Darby slipping into bed next to him, wonderfully nude. Perhaps she was just as needy as he was and had made the first move.

He blinked open his eyes, the room around him blurry as he sought out his seductress. Then his sight settled on a pair of brown eyes with slitty pupils...and he got a blast of the nastiest breath he'd ever smelled.

Darby wasn't running her fingers through his hair. Rather, Billy the Goat was licking his hair.

He sprung from the bed so fast he was lucky he didn't pull a muscle.

Billy bleated in protest.

"*You're* upset?" he muttered, running his hand over his hair and the saliva coating it. "Try to imagine how *I* feel."

He heard giggling by the door. He swung around to see Erin and Lindy trying to hold in their laughter as Billy rounded the bed and came after John, the bell around his neck clanging. John caught the goat's lead and pointed a finger at the mischievous twins. "Payback's...well, not very much fun. For you two."

Over the past three days he'd suffered myriad practical jokes, from shaving cream in his boots, to cat hair in his comb and gravel in his bed. This, however, was the first time he'd had to contend with a live animal licking his person.

The war the girls had waged against him was escalating. And it was past time he entered it.

His eyes began to water. He rubbed the back of his hand against his nose, then gave a sneeze that rocked him on his feet.

"Oh, my God!" Darby stepped hesitantly into the doorway, slapping her hand over her mouth as she took in the scene. The girls made a beeline to pass her, but she caught both of them by the shoulders. "What's going on here?"

John grimaced, sidestepping a charge by Billy. "Let's just say I won't have to wash my face this morning. Billy saw to that for me."

"He didn't lick your face," Erin said. "He was eating your hair."

Lindy began giggling again, setting off a fresh round of laughter at John's expense. Even Darby appeared to be having a tough time keeping a straight face. John grimaced at her.

"Erin, go get Billy, please, and take him back outside," Darby turned the six-year-old toward the goat. "Lindy, you help."

Suddenly the laughter stopped and the twins mumbled protests as they trudged toward John. He all too happily handed them the goat's lead.

The clump-clump of hooves on the stairs sounded; John gave a sigh of relief, and Darby smiled at him.

John couldn't help a smile of his own now that the incident had passed. "Don't tell me, I took Billy's room and he's out to get me for it?"

"Not exactly."

"Tell me you weren't in on this."

"I wasn't in on this."

"Why doesn't that make me feel better?" John reached for a towel on top of a pile Darby had put on the dresser for him. "Yeah, well, if you'll excuse me, I have to go wash goat gunk out of my hair."

Darby apparently gave in to temptation, and her laughter filled the room.

"Sure, go ahead and laugh," he said. "You weren't the one who woke up expecting to find a sexy woman sneaking into bed with you only to get blasted by goat breath. Add my allergies on top of it and you wouldn't be laughing, either."

Darby made an effort to stop. "Well, at least I won't ever have to worry about morning breath with you, will I."

Heat, sure and strong, swept through John. Her comment seemed to indicate that he *would* get the opportunity to wake up in the same bed with her. The prospect brought every one of the naughty images from his dream back to him tenfold. "Darby, your breath could be twice as bad as that goat's and I'd never say anything."

The smile eased from her face, replaced by a weightier expression that left no doubt that her mind was traveling down the same path as his.

Three days, and he hadn't had a single opportunity to continue his campaign to win her hand. Well, okay, maybe there had been a couple. But he'd been caught so off guard he hadn't been able to take advantage of them. Dealing with the new living arrangements, the nonstop shenanigans of the twins and his constant state of arousal whenever Darby was within touching distance was enough to knock any man off-kilter.

Downstairs the back door slammed. Darby averted her gaze. "Um, coffee's ready and breakfast should be done in a few. See you downstairs?"

He'd rather see her in his bed. But considering the

state of his hair, he didn't think it was a good idea to make a move just now.

"Um, yeah. See you downstairs."

Later that morning John wondered if standing on the alien surface of Mars would feel the same as watching the ultrasound screen at Old Orchard General Hospital.

"See, there's the baby's head," the doctor was saying. He didn't quite catch her full name. Something Barnaby. She was new here, and he'd never met her before.

Darby reached for John's hand and squeezed. He looked at her face, finding it full of joy and hope and brightness. He couldn't help but smile when all he really wanted to do was bolt for the door.

"Would you like a video of the session?" the doctor asked as she switched off the machinery and rubbed the goop from Darby's stomach with a paper towel. The slightest of swells rounded the surface, something he hadn't noticed until watching the ultrasound and seeing the baby, his baby, in there. It seemed uncomfortably intimate, somehow, witnessing Darby's examination. Strange, since they'd been very intimate and he hadn't felt any discomfort then.

He cleared his throat. "Can you tell what sex it is?"

The doctor smiled. "Are you sure you want to know?"

"No," Darby said, giving him a stern glance. "No, we don't want to know."

He grimaced. He wanted to know. Wanted to be

able to refer to the baby as he or she, rather than the anonymous it.

"Can you tell just me?" he asked.

The doctor told Darby she could get up. "I think that's something you'll want to discuss with your wife first."

John locked gazes with Darby. His wife. The words sounded weird coming from the young obstetrician's mouth, yet somehow right.

Darby, on the other hand, looked ready to jump out of her skin. "We're not, um, married," she said.

"Yet," John added.

The doctor merely smiled. "Then I think it's doubly important that you two talk about the sex issue." She wrote something down in her file. "If one parent finds out, it's a pretty good bet both parents will know, regardless of his or her wishes."

John bristled. "I can keep a secret."

Darby laughed quietly. "Yeah, like you wouldn't tell the entire town if you knew it was a boy."

"Is it a boy?" John asked the doctor, the whole prospect of his having a child growing more real to him.

She wagged her finger at him. "Talk to your…er, to Darby if you want to find out."

He grinned at Darby. She shook her head.

Just another thing he was going to have to bring her to her senses about.

How, exactly, did a guy go about seducing a woman he was already living with? That was the question that plagued John throughout the remainder of the day on the job. The twins...well, their presence proved a challenge he hadn't thought of when he'd agreed to move in. Erin and Lindy were more alert than nearly all his deputies combined.

Except for Cole, of course, who seemed to be one step ahead of him more often than not as of late.

"Your unannounced opponent for this year's election, Bully Wentworth, had a few choice words to say about the integrity of the office in this morning's paper," Cole was saying, leaning on the doorjamb. "He didn't come right out and say anything about your...situation with the Widow Conrad, but he didn't have to. It's all right there, between the lines."

John sat back in his chair, wincing at Cole's calling Darby the Widow Conrad. "Shocker, seeing as his father owns the paper."

Cole grinned. "I think you should ask for space for a response."

"Yeah, and they'd give me two lines between advertisements for fertilizer and feminine products. No, thank you."

Cole straightened from the doorjamb. "You have to offer some sort of response, John. Surely you can't plan to sit back and do nothing. You have to defend yourself."

"Who says?"

"I do, for one."

"Besides you."

Cole took a long sip of his coffee. "Nearly half the population. I can't seem to go anywhere without someone asking me about what's happening with you and what you have to say about Wentworth's accusations.''

''That makes two of us, but since when does gossip have anything to do with the sheriff's office?''

''Since townsfolk are calling in fake reports just to get one of us out there in hopes of getting a scoop.''

John lifted his brows. ''That's happening?''

''Yeah. Just this morning Jugawatt called in a possible intruder alert. The intruder was a bird.''

''No.''

''Yes.''

John sighed and rubbed his face, wondering when things would start getting easier, instead of more complicated. From some of the townsfolk, especially the guys, he got thumbs-up signs. When Dusty heard the news, he'd nearly threatened to blacken his other eye. But it was the reaction from the women in town that puzzled him. A few looked at him with downright hostility. Others seemed to size him up, as if the news cast him in a new light and had them wondering what he could do for them.

Yeah, invite the sheriff out to do some tasks around the house and he'll satisfy all your needs.

Ouch.

''Threaten to arrest anyone who calls in a false report from here on in,'' he said.

''That'll help in your reelection campaign.''

''What campaign?'' he said under his breath, not expecting Cole to answer.

''The one Mrs. Noonan's heading up, along with the Old Orchard Women's Club.''

Good Lord. ''You're kidding?''

"Nope. They've posted signs in Penelope Moon's window and everything. Put them up this morning. Though I think connecting that wacko to you may not be in your best interests."

"Penelope's not a wacko," John said in defense of the New Age shop owner he'd gone to school with. "She's just...different."

"And different is just what you don't want right now. You want to make yourself one of the people. Of the people, by the people, for the people, that kind of thing."

John pulled a file in front of him and reached for the phone. "What, are you putting a bid in as my campaign manager? Assuming there's going to be a campaign. Which I haven't said one way or another that there is."

Cole shrugged. "Just trying to help."

Distantly John realized he was being a little tough on the young deputy, but he couldn't help himself. He couldn't deal with this one more thing heaped on top of everything else at the moment.

"Yeah, I know," he said gruffly. "Thanks."

Cole took that as his cue to leave, and John buried his face in his hands. The saying "When it rains it pours" certainly held true here. He glanced at his watch, Darby slipping into his thoughts again. He wondered if she wouldn't mind having her mother keep the twins for the night so he could at least make some progress in one aspect of his life. The problem with that was he had the feeling Darby was using the girls to keep him at arm's length and might even see his asking to get rid of the girls as another reason she shouldn't marry him. After all, he couldn't ask her to ship the kids out every time he wanted to sleep with her. Especially since that was the sorry state he was in every moment of every day.

No. Instead, he would have to find a way to get a handle on the girls, work around them and plant a bull's-eye directly on Darby's back.

And this Saturday morning would be the perfect time to do that. If he could wait two more days.

''Sheriff?''

''What?'' he barked, dropping his hands to the desk in frustration.

Only, instead of Cole, he found himself staring at the questioning face of Pastor Jonas Noble.

Great. Just great. That was all he needed now....

''Pastor Jonas really told you that either we should get married or you should move out?'' Darby asked that Saturday morning, comfortable if not particularly attractive in her flowered capri pants and pink T-shirt. Attractive wasn't what she was going for, anyway, she reminded herself as she led the way into the barn, John following on her heels. In fact, she'd gone out of her way to make herself as unattractive as possible since he'd moved in. She wore little if no makeup. Donned her oldest and ugliest clothing. And if worse came to worst, she kept the twins firmly between her and the man who made her want to leap into bed with him every time she met his gaze and felt that hum of attraction arc between them.

The problem was that now the twins were some-where out in the back field playing with Ellie Johansen, Dusty and Jolie's foster child. Darby hadn't made the play date, John had. She had little doubt, however, that Jolie was more than a willing conspirator. Despite how tough the fire chief was, she had a romantic streak a mile wide. And never passed up the opportunity to remind Darby that nearly a year had passed since Erick's death and it was time she moved on with her life.

She thought of the baby growing within her and wondered how much more quickly she could move.

"Yeah, it wasn't pretty," John said, and Darby realized he was still talking about Pastor Jonas. "Though I got the impression he really wasn't all that concerned with our living arrangements. It was like he felt obligated to say the words, but wasn't in complete agreement with the meaning. Odd, considering his position. I would have thought he'd quote scripture or something to back up his position. Where do you want these?"

"Over there is fine." Darby motioned toward a stack of hay bales and he put down his load. Only Sheriff John Sparks could pull off looking masculine while holding dainty wicker baskets.

"You know, several people have said things like that. Ever since Pastor Adams came back from his pilgrimage and asked Pastor Jonas to stay and take over some of his responsibilities permanently, more parishioners than not come away from counseling more confused than when they went in." She pushed a strand of hair from her eyes. "He actually told Elva Mollenkopf that she should speak her mind whenever she was moved to."

"Maybe he was trying some twisted sort of reverse psychology." John grimaced, likely thinking of the thoughtless woman whose razor-sharp tongue had injured many, Darby included. "I hope it works. We have a running bet around the office on how long it will take before someone snaps and runs Elva over with their car."

"You do not."

"Okay, we don't." He grinned. "But we should."

Darby smiled as she picked up one of the baskets and headed for the barn's back door. John hesitantly followed and she surreptitiously turned to watch him. He was looking around the barn as if he'd just stepped into a parallel but different universe.

John's being uncomfortable in rural surroundings was exactly what she'd been banking on. Over the past five days he had come to fit in more than she had imagined, adding a warmth to the household that found her frequently thinking of him as a permanent addition. Which was exactly what she didn't want. This morning, she planned to make him see that he didn't belong here. That they didn't belong together. He tripped over a thick rope, and she stopped herself from asking if he was all right. And if she helped herself believe that he didn't belong here, well, all the better.

So far he'd proved himself more than capable in everything. He'd even taken Billy's tongue bath the other day in stride. And the twins... No matter how incorrigible they were, he somehow always managed to diffuse the situation in a way that left everybody feeling good. Including her. So much so that she actually found herself imagining what life would be like if he was here permanently.

Darby nearly tripped over another length of rope.

"Are you all right?"

She swallowed hard. "Yes…I'm fine." Or at least she would be once she'd convinced him that he didn't really want to marry her and he left the farm once and for all. "The, um, chicken coop is out the back way. I positioned it that way so the twins wouldn't have free access." She unlocked and opened the door. "Of course if you'd rather wake up to chickens pecking you on the cheek, just let me know."

"I think I'll pass, thank you."

She motioned for him to go ahead of her. "I thought you'd say that."

He turned, the small confines of the coop putting him chest to chest with her. "Of course should I wake up to find you pecking my cheek…well, I'd have no objections to that."

Maybe this hadn't been such a good idea, after all, Darby thought, absently wetting her lips with her tongue. His gaze followed the movement, making the ball of awareness in her chest dip lower. Much lower.

"I've never, um, collected eggs before," he said.

Darby thrust the basket at him, using it as a buffer between them. "Well, if you're going to be staying here, you'd better learn."

His eyes narrowed on her face as if trying to read the motivation behind her words. Darby turned toward the row of chickens to her left and positioned the other basket in front of her. "You get the other side."

''Okay,'' he said slowly.

When she sensed he had finally turned his attention away from her, she took a deep breath. That was a close one. Perhaps she should have rescheduled her farm lesson for a time when the twins could be with them. She looked through the chicken wire, catching sight of the twins in question, playing hide-and-seek with little Ellie in a thatch of trees some fifty yards away. She slanted a glance at John, finding him trying to shoo a chicken away from her straw nest. The chicken squawked and pecked at his hand. He shook it, stared at the offending chicken, then tried again with much the same result. After four such attempts, he finally managed to get under the chicken and retrieve the one egg that waited there.

John caught her watching him and growled low in his throat. ''What do you think of poultry for dinner?''

Darby finally gave in and laughed so hard she nearly dropped the half-dozen eggs in her own basket.

''What's so damn funny?'' he asked.

She pointed at him, trying to straighten from being doubled up holding her side. ''You are.''

His dark expression helped her get control of herself. She guessed it wasn't often that Sheriff John Sparks found himself in a situation he didn't know how to handle.

''Here, let me show you the secret to getting the eggs without getting your hand pecked off.''

She ignored the little voice in her head that told her she wasn't supposed to be helping him and stepped closer. ''Here,'' she said, taking his hand.

The instant her skin made contact with his, she felt a spark of electricity that traveled the length of her arm and back again. She cleared her throat. "You move the chicken like so," she said, her voice hoarse. "Then you sneak the egg right out from under them." She guided his hand, seeing his amazement that the chicken didn't launch an all-out attack. She cleared her throat. "Okay?"

He put the egg in the basket. "You could have saved me a lot of trouble by telling me how to do it in the first place."

"Yes, but then I would have missed out on the fun."

Suddenly all amusement vanished from John's handsome face, replaced by an intensity that filled her with heat. His pupils dilated, his throat worked around a swallow, and then he was reaching for her. Darby's breath caught in her throat as his hands settled on her hips, then dragged her nearer to him so that only mere millimeters separated them. She took a deep breath, the move putting the tips of her breasts into direct contact with the hard wall of his chest.

"We're, um, supposed to be working."

"Oh?" John said. "I think I deserve a reward for what you just put me through. Better yet, incentive."

Then John was doing the one thing Darby sensed he always had control over. He was kissing her. Thoroughly. Passionately. Hungrily. His tongue melding with hers, then retreating, his fingers softly stroking her hips through her pants, then hauling her against him, pressing his arousal against her belly. She gasped, all heat and fire, her bones dissolving under the skill of his onslaught.

Dear Lord, this wasn't going at all the way she'd planned....

## *Chapter Ten*

Boy, this was even better than he'd hoped.

John deepened the kiss, filled with the urgent desire to inhale Darby and all she embodied. She was, in that moment, everything he wanted in the world. He couldn't think of a single place he'd rather be than right here, holding her, kissing her. Feeling her body leaning into his. Feeling the promise of a more intimate meeting grow with each beat of his heart.

"Holy cow," Darby whispered, laying her cheek against his, her fingers digging into his back.

He chuckled softly. "Please tell me you don't have any cows."

She drew back and looked at him, a smile in her green eyes. "No cows."

"Good."

"Not yet."

Her words seemed to imply that he would still be around when and if she decided to add to her menagerie. A slip? Or a subconscious wish she had yet to realize?

He groaned and pulled her back for another kiss. The humming sound she made wound around him like a velvet cord, drawing him closer to her in a way he'd never been to anyone else. He moved his hand up to cup a soft breast. Her ragged moan increased his heat quotient by ten so that his arousal throbbed against her stomach, begging for a deeper, more meaningful connection.

"I want you. Now," he whispered roughly, backing her toward the door to the barn, then swiveling her inside. He closed the barrier, then pushed her up against it, his actions braver than when they were out in the open, the girls in view. He pushed her shirt up and freed a ripe breast, fastening his mouth around a delectably erect crest even as her own hand sought and found his erection under the denim of his jeans. He quickly realized that the control he'd been seeking by kissing her to begin with was literally shifting hands, putting her firmly in the driver's seat. He blinked to look into her eyes, finding that she liked things that way. She popped the button on the fly of his jeans, slid her fingers inside and began stroking. He nearly roared with longing as she rubbed the moist top of his erection, then brought her fingers to her mouth and sucked.

"You're going to end me right here and now," he said under his breath, unzipping her pants and tugging them down over her hips and legs. She eagerly stepped out of them, then lifted her arms for him to tear off her shirt. Then he thrust her against the door, wrapping her legs around his waist. A couple of moves and his arousal rested promisingly against her slick opening

John purposely held back from breaking the threshold as he sought and held her gaze. "Darby?"

She restlessly wet her lips, her green eyes almost black in the dim interior of the barn. "Hmm?"

She tilted her hips and sought his erection with her hands, intent on forcing him to continue. He caught those hands and pulled them up above her head and held them there. His gaze wandered down her gloriously naked body, pausing at her breasts, heaving with her labored breathing, then down to where her silky wedge of hair tangled with his.

He met her gaze again, using every ounce of willpower he possessed not to thrust into her to the hilt. "Marry me," he whispered.

Her breathing hitched and he fit the tip of his arousal against her more tightly, a small move all that was needed to breach the entrance.

"No," she whispered, making that small move. Now she surrounded him, pulsing, squeezing, hot and wet.

John's groan was as much a result of her response as it was his response to her wanton moves. He released her wrists and snaked his hands around to her bottom, finding and following the shallow crevice from behind, opening her further to him as he pulled back and thrust deeply.

"Yes," she moaned without shame, digging her fingers into his shoulders. "Oh, yes."

John thrust again and again, deeper and deeper, until he could go no farther, feeling the shuddering of her slick muscles as she climaxed, vowing to get her to say yes to his proposal with the same veracity that she welcomed him into her body. He bent his knees, balancing her on his upper thighs, then thrust his hips up, bringing her down on his pulsing shaft even farther. She exploded around him again, and this time he allowed himself to travel at warp speed down that swirling, twirling tunnel of color and pure sensation, marveling at the richness of it, the overwhelming, humbling nature of it.

They stayed like that for long minutes, neither of them moving but for their breathing, their skin saturated with sweat, moved beyond words and sharing something no one could consciously give.

A sound slowly penetrated the fog that acted as a buffer between them and the rest of the world, followed by children laughing. Darby's muscles tightened where she still surrounded him and John groaned softly, wanting the world to go away again so he could—

"The girls," she whispered fiercely. "They're coming."

They weren't the only ones, John thought, fighting to regain control even as his hips unconsciously bucked under her.

Darby gasped, her eyes full of passion as she met his gaze. Then she wriggled until he was forced to withdraw from her dripping wetness. Her feet were on the ground and in a flash she was dressed. He still fumbled with the fly of his jeans.

''Mom?'' a young voice called out, and the door on the opposite side of the barn opened, inviting a thick shaft of bright sunlight to play with the dust motes in the dim interior.

Darby smoothed back her hair and opened the door to the chicken coop that they had put to better use, pulling John with her. She looked very much like a woman who had just been thoroughly made love to. Her color was high. Her lips marvelously swollen, her eyes bright. And just looking at her made John want to drive the twins to Jolie and Dusty's for the weekend, so that he could have his fill of this generous woman.

''Mom?'' The voice was closer now, and Erin's tawny head popped into the opening.

''What is it, Erin?'' Darby asked, feigning normalcy.

Erin looked at John, her eyes narrowing as if she knew what they'd been doing and didn't approve.

''The phone was ringing and Lindy picked it up.''

John remembered the cordless that Darby had put on the steps outside the house.

''It's for Uncle Sparky.''

Darby ran her hand over her tousled hair for the sixth time in as many minutes, still internally shattered by John's amorous attentions in the barn and the fact that they were nearly caught by the twins and Ellie. Which was stupid, she told herself. She need not be worried. She was an adult capable of making her own decisions. And oh, how right the one in the barn had been! Blood still surged hotly through her veins, making her even more aware of the man she had vowed to stay away from.

She stood at the kitchen sink, washing juice glasses and discreetly listening in on John's conversation just outside the screen door.

"That's impossible. How could they have escaped?"

Escaped? A thrill of fear raced across Darby's skin. She finished the glasses, then put a plate of cookies on the table as a snack for the three girls, who were listening as avidly to John's conversation as she was. Ellie said something about oatmeal cookies being her favorite and Erin shushed her.

"Put out an APB. Now," John ordered, cursing a blue streak that raised even Darby's brows. "I'll be at the office in ten."

Darby watched as he disconnected the line, then shot into the house and grabbed his keys from where they hung next to hers near the door. He blinked at her, then the girls, as if just realizing they were there.

"I, um, have to go."

"What's wrong Sheriff John?" Ellie asked, all innocent blue eyes and trembling, crumb-coated lips.

John held Darby's gaze for a moment longer, then his eyes softened as he looked at the five-year-old. The little girl had lost her mother in a fire six months ago, and her father was going through rehabilitation after suffering significant burns to a good portion of his body while trying to save his young family. John stepped over to the girl and laid his large hand on her skinny shoulder, then tousled her hair. "Nothing I can't handle, kiddo." He got a faraway look on his face. "Nothing I can't handle."

Darby had her arms wrapped around herself, warding off a chill that had nothing to do with the temperature.

"I'll call you from the office later," he said, crossing to stand in front of Darby.

She nodded. He didn't say he'd be home later. Didn't offer an explanation of why he was going to the office. She shuddered and hugged herself more tightly, all too familiar with the MO. Lord knows she'd gone through it enough times with Erick.

"Okay," she croaked, though she felt anything but okay.

John looked puzzled. Then he leaned forward and pressed a soft kiss to her cheek. Ellie giggled, the twins shifted restlessly, and Darby felt her skin heat to the roots of her hair. He rested his hand on the side of her neck, his thumb lightly caressing her. "Everything will be fine, Darby."

She nodded, but she didn't buy the words for a minute.

"I'll explain everything when I get home."

Her heart skipped a beat, the words a remarkable crack in the normal routine. Erick had never said he'd explain things. Had rarely shared anything about his job as a firefighter with her. It had frustrated her, often made her feel locked out of an important part of his life. And the phone call today had brought all that back tenfold. Simply because John didn't say much to her about his job as the sheriff, either.

She smiled and nodded again.

Then he was gone.

And Darby's hand slid absently to her stomach, as if to protect the baby there.

Fifteen minutes later John parked his Jeep behind a paramedic truck, then stormed into the sheriff's office, his breathing irregular, sweat coating the back of his neck, his mind splintered between what he'd been told on the phone and Darby's reaction to his being called away.

She'd looked shocked, afraid and heartbroken. And John had known a moment of pause, remembering what she'd gone through before with Erick. Watching her husband leave for a run. Then getting the phone call saying he would never come home again. John hated that, however inadvertently, he was putting her through that again.

''Somebody tell me what's going on,'' he ordered, bypassing Cole, who stood at the counter in full uniform, and advancing on Ed Hanover, who sat in his usual chair looking anything but usual. A fire-department paramedic was dabbing the back of the older man's head with a thick wad of cotton, bringing away gobs of blood.

Cole motioned toward his co-worker. ''I checked in about half an hour ago after I couldn't raise an answer here and found Ed knocked out cold in one of the holding cells.''

Ed grimaced, his too-thin body wincing away from the paramedic's hand. ''Ow, that hurts.''

The young paramedic sighed. ''Deputy Hanover,

I'm going to have to ask you to come to the hospital. You're going to need some stitches. I also need to make sure you're not suffering from a concussion."

Ed tried to wave him away. "I've had worse than this little ding, boy. If you feel around enough, you'll find the metal plate in there, a souvenir from my second of two tours in Nam."

"Just the same…"

John held his impatience in check. "Ed?"

The older man blinked up at him. "Sorry, Sparky. I really don't know what hit me. One minute I was back there picking up the breakfast dishes, the next I woke up to find Cole's ugly mug staring down at me."

Cole held up a mutilated fork, two prongs bent out of place. "They must have used this to jimmy the locks," he said. "And ambushed Ed when he turned his back."

Ed swiped at a spot of food on his shirt. "Look, my uniform is ruined. And I didn't even get to enjoy the food that ruined it."

"Forget the uniform, Ed." John checked his watch. "What time did you go back there?"

Ed shrugged. "I can't be sure exactly. About nine? Maybe it was closer to nine-fifteen?"

The prisoners should have been fed at about eight.

Ed cursed and moved away from the paramedic again. "I had some things to do before I went back to clean up the breakfast plates."

John paced restlessly across the office. Had Ed gone back immediately, as he should have, he would have known a fork was missing from one of the trays, and the twosome would never have had a chance to use the pilfered fork on the locks.

It was nearly eleven now. Which meant the escapees had a good two-hour jump on them.

John abruptly turned away from the counter again before moving to stand in front of the window that overlooked the street. He gazed out at the slice of Old Orchard that he could see. The Hamiltons, a young family, were coming out of the rebuilt General Store with bags of groceries, while Old Man Jake swept the front sidewalk and stopped to talk to them. Elva Mollenkopf was out terrorizing the community at large, coming out of one shop and going into another, her face pinched, her eyes piercing as she sought out her next victim. Penelope Moon was decorating the front of her shop for Easter, placing egg decals around a Keep Sparks as Sheriff poster that sported a picture of him. He cringed and turned from the scene, wondering what the street would look like if the townsfolk knew there were two hardcore criminals out there somewhere. Criminals he'd been in charge of. Criminals capable of anything. Armed criminals. John didn't have to ask if they'd taken Ed's gun. That was a given.

Damn. Damn. Damn.

He turned toward the men. "Cole, get on the horn with everyone you can think of and recruit them for the manhunt. Then I want you out on the west county border between Peterson's pumpkin patch and the McCrearys'. Send Brady out to cover Route 108. I'm going to call the U.S. Marshal Service and inform them of the break, then head to the police station and pull them in on the hunt.''

"Yes, sir.'' Cole shot into action, pulling the phone forward and popping open the Rolodex. John looked down at his oxford shirt and jeans, surprised to find he wasn't in uniform. Then he remembered why he wasn't. He looked up to meet Ed's gaze. The older man had gone silent, his eyes full of apology, his thin hand reaching for and touching his empty gun holster. "They got my gun, Sparky. They got my gun.''

John felt a stab of sympathy. Given Ed's military past, John guessed that the impact on Ed of loss of a firearm was significant.

"I don't know what to say, Sparky. Nothing like this has ever happened to me. I'm sorry as hell. I dropped the ball.''

John continued to look at him. "We all do sometimes, Ed. We all do.'' But now it was *his* job to pick the ball back up and run with it. That is, if he could find it. "You get to the hospital and get that wound looked after. Then if you can, get back here and start making calls to the perimeter farms and ask if they've seen anything out of the ordinary.''

"We'll do,'' Ed said with renewed energy, visibly relieved. And John knew it wasn't because his job was safe. The man was genuinely upset that he had caused so much trouble and was grateful for John's forgiveness.

John strode into his office, picked up the address book for the numbers of the neighboring counties' sheriff's offices, then hurried out the door and into his Jeep.

He only hoped he wasn't too late.

* * *

By ten o'clock that night, Darby had cleaned the farmhouse from top to bottom and was contemplating the two criminals John had found camping out at Old Violet Jenkins's place. She and Jolie knew that John would blame himself for their escape this morning and would work until he dropped trying to bring them back in.

Merely hearing his voice had amplified her need to see him, to make sure he was all right. So she'd prepared a dinner plate filled with his favorites and piled the girls into the car with the promise of an ice-cream cone, then driven to the sheriff's office. Only, he wasn't there. Instead, she'd talked to Ed, who was sporting half a roll of gauze on his head, then had been forced to leave the plate for when John might return, along with a note saying she would wait up for him. She'd wanted to add a request that he be careful, but remembered Erick hating when she'd said that and left it off.

Her arms filled, she inched open the door to the girls' room. There were four bedrooms, enough for each of them to have her own room, but they preferred to share, unquestionably connected by that special bond that twins are said to have. The light from the hall fell across the beds, revealing that the girls were in the same positions they had been in when she'd last checked. Darby stood there for a long moment, gazing at them. She knew how John's exit that morning had affected her. She could only imagine what it had done to the girls.

Despite all their inventive attempts to alienate John, there was no doubt in Darby's mind that they loved him. Always had. What was there not to love? His pursuing dangerous criminals had to bring the loss of their father back to them as much as it did to her.

Darby quietly closed the door and then walked down the hall to her room, dumping the contents of her arms on top of her bed. Her big, forlorn-looking, empty bed. One by one, she put the items she'd brought upstairs away, then fingered through the videos she had under the television across from the bed, searching for something to take her mind off her fears. Finding a romantic comedy, she pushed the button to eject the tape that was in there. She slid the video out and glanced at the label, her breath catching when she realized it was home video footage of Erick that she had watched endlessly in the weeks following his death. Her fingers tightened around the cold plastic as if touching something he had touched might bring a direct connection with him, through which he could tell her what she should do, where she should go from there. A line through which she could tell him how very sorry she was for having betrayed him with his best friend.

Moisture blurring her vision, she slid the video into its case, fingering the raised lettering she'd used to label it. Moments later she forced herself to put it with the other videos. The long row toppled over like a line of dominoes, revealing a handheld two-way radio just behind them.

How odd. It looked just like one of a pair Erick had given to the girls for their birthday. She picked up the fluorescent-blue radio, finding the talk button pushed all the way in and the radio on. She released the button, then turned the power switch off and shook out the dead batteries. How long had it been there? There was no possible way for her to tell. She replaced the batteries with a pair she found in the nightstand drawer, then put it on top where she immediately forgot it. Instead, she reached for the phone, began dialing the number for John's office, then disconnected halfway through. He had enough to worry about without adding her concerns to the list. Instead, she wondered where he was right now, whether he'd eaten the dinner she'd taken him, and if he had thought about her at all throughout the day. On the heels of those thoughts came the memories of their activities in the barn. She swallowed thickly, then stretched across her big, empty bed, wishing he was there.

Even if she could never marry John, the connection between them was undeniable. A link she couldn't seem to sever no matter how hard she tried. It existed on a physical level, but also went much, much deeper. Deeper than she could ever hope to reach and rip out. She felt him all the way down to her bones. Heard his sexy chuckle when he wasn't around. Saw his handsome grin whenever she closed her eyes.

She turned her head restlessly, looking for the television remote control. Thinking about him wasn't going to make the waiting any easier. But instead of the remote, her gaze was drawn again to the walkie-talkie. Absently she reached out and switched it on.

She wondered why neither of the girls had said anything about it being missing.

She stared at the ceiling, listening to the quiet hissing of the radio, searching for some sort of pattern in the white noise.

"Daddy? Daddy, this is Lindy. Please answer me, Daddy."

Darby was so startled she shot up off the bed, her heart thudding wildly. She recognized the quiet desperation in her daughter's voice, the unmistakable sadness.

"Daddy?" A soft sniffle. "Why won't you talk to me anymore? I'm sorry if I was a bad girl. I promise, I'll never be bad again."

Darby fumbled for the radio, nearly knocking it from the bedside table as she picked it up and turned the volume down. "Daddy, when are you coming back? Erin and me need you."

Dear Lord. Darby's heart gave such a tremendous squeeze she nearly sobbed aloud. She remembered Erin's outburst when she'd overheard John's first proposal. Her insistence that her father was coming back. Both twins' refusal to discuss the matter with her.

Obviously they thought they could communicate with Erick through the radio.

She caught her breath as she put the pieces together. The radio being on and stuck behind the videos under the television in the talk position. Her watching home footage of Erick over and over again many a night after his death. Apparently at some point the girls must have had their radio on and heard their father's voice filter through the tiny speaker, thinking he was trying to communicate with them.

She stared at the tiny object. Until the batteries went dead.

How long had the twins been trying to talk to their father? And how had she gone so long without knowing what they were doing?

"Daddy?" She heard the tears in Lindy's voice. "Daddy, please say something to me."

Gripping the radio so tightly in her hands she was afraid she might break it, Darby grappled for what to do. She turned toward the door, but it seemed to take Herculean effort to force herself to walk toward it and tiptoe into and down the hall. A turn of a knob and the door to the twins' room opened. Erin was still sound asleep. But Lindy's bed was now empty, the sheets showing the outline of where her small body had been. Darby touched the soft cotton, finding it still warm, then looked under the beds. Not there. She checked under the desk, then beside the bookcase, then came to a stop before the closet.

"I love you, Daddy," Lindy's muffled, sobbing voice filtered through the thick wood.

Darby tore the door open and dropped to her knees, gathering a sobbing Lindy into her aching arms. "Oh, baby. I'm so, so sorry."

## *Chapter Eleven*

John was still questioning whether he should have gone to his trailer, instead of to Darby's. It was three o'clock in the morning. He was no closer to finding the two fugitives than he'd been when he'd gotten the call this morning. His head felt so heavy he could barely hold it upright. He'd finally been forced to hand the search off to his deputies and local and state police for a few hours of much-needed shut-eye. The moment he decided that, all he'd been able to think about was getting to Darby. Seeing her again. Knowing that she and the twins were all right.

He walked around the living room of the old farmhouse, switching off lights as he went. The house looked warm and inviting, not like everyone was asleep. But the absence of sound told him everyone probably was.

He slipped off his shoes and put them on the steps, then climbed to the second floor. A check of the twins found them both tucked in and sleeping. He eyed the door slightly ajar at the end of the hall, the door to Darby's room. The light was on in there. Glancing toward the guest bedroom, he headed instead toward the light.

The lightest push with his hand made the door swing open and allowed him to gaze upon the woman who had occupied his thoughts ceaselessly today. She was still fully dressed and curled up on her side on top of the covers. He dared to step closer and saw her clutching what looked like one of those kid's walkie-talkies. He frowned and eased it from her hand, turning it over, then putting it on the table beside the bed.

Damn, but she was beautiful. Her curly brown hair lay in soft waves on the snow-white pillow behind her, a stray lock curving against her cheek. He reached out and brushed it aside with the back of his knuckles, marveling at the butter softness of her skin. Flawless. Perfect. Just like the woman herself.

Occasionally his brothers joked about their spouses' many flaws. When John protested, they always felt compelled to warn him. ''Just wait until you get married. You'll see what we're talking about.'' Only after a few days with Darby, he had yet to figure out what they meant. He couldn't imagine seeing any flaw in the woman lying asleep across the bed.

He gently sat down on the mattress, careful not to wake her. He just needed to hold her. Once. Feel her body next to his. He promised himself he wouldn't do it for long. He intended to honor her request that they not sleep together in the house. Well, at least he'd be honorable while she was unconscious. It was, after all, the gentlemanly thing to do.

Problem was, he wasn't feeling real gentlemanly right now. He was feeling selfish. He wanted to feel her body snuggled close to his. Breathe in the sweet scent of her hair. Press his lips to her silken skin.

And that was exactly what he did. He stretched out, moving the bed as little as possible, and slid toward her. Darby seemed to sense his heat and shifted the remainder of the way, making a soft humming sound as she curled up to his side, laying her head on his shoulder.

John stayed as still as possible, afraid she might wake up and realize what he'd done and send him away. When she didn't, he pressed his hand against her back. She made a soft sound and tilted her head. Now he could see directly into her face. He eyed her moist lips. Her smooth brow. Then caught a glimpse of faint streaks under her eyes. Had she been crying? He guessed she had. He groaned and held her closer.

He was surprised by the pain he felt at the thought of her hurting for any reason. She shifted again, then her green eyes blinked open. He held his breath, watching her gaze at him with sleepy eyes. Then she gave him the faintest of smiles and closed her eyes again.

John swallowed hard. Oh, boy. While he'd always known he'd felt something…different for Darby Parker Conrad, he'd had no idea of the breadth and depth of it. But now it consumed him, filling him to overflowing. Made him feel a part of something, yet adrift.

But was what he felt love? What he felt was so complicated he was afraid it would take him a lifetime to figure it out.

He carefully shifted the woman at his side, reached for a blanket at the foot of the bed and covered them both. He only hoped Darby would agree to *give* him that lifetime.

He settled back and closed his eyes, absorbing everything that was Darby, her scent, her body, her spirit. He'd only lie there for a few moments. Just enough to drink in his fill of her, he told himself.

Then the world faded to black.

Darby awoke slowly, feeling magnificently reluctant to do so. Her dreams were filled with images of lying next to John, his warm body touching hers, his arms holding her. She opened her eyes and gazed out the window just as the sun was breaking the horizon, and realized she hadn't been dreaming. John was next to her. Or, more accurately, behind her, his body spooned around hers. Before she allowed panic to settle in, she snuggled a little more firmly against him, covering his hand where it was draped across her hip with hers. This, she could definitely get used to.

The sound of movement in the other room brought her eyes open again. The twins.

Her heart gave a painful squeeze before she could even recall the incident with the two-way radio. Dear, poor Lindy. Her little girl had been sobbing her heart out all alone in that closet, gripping the radio in her hands as if her life depended on her contacting her father. Darby hadn't known what to say. So instead, she'd gathered her trembling daughter's body against hers and just held her.

They both sat on that cold closet floor for nearly an hour. Darby rocking, moved beyond words. And what could she have said? She didn't think reminding her daughter that her daddy was gone and wasn't coming back would have helped at that moment. Especially if what she suspected was correct and the girls had heard Erick's voice via the videotape through the radio after she'd told them of his death. She would have to figure out something to do, some action to take. But just then she'd needed to reassure Lindy that she loved her. And that her daddy had loved her. That she hadn't done anything wrong, wasn't the cause of his death or his eternal silence.

She reluctantly moved to slide from John's warm embrace only to feel his grip on her hip tighten, refusing her escape. She turned her head and found him gazing at her calmly.

"You're awake," she said.

"So are you."

She settled back in against him, turning her head away. She heard the sound of the toilet flushing down the hall, followed by footsteps moving away from her door. She guessed that one of the girls had used the bathroom and was stumbling back to her room.

"What time did you get in last night?"

"Three o'clock this morning."

She bit her bottom lip, trying to suppress the desire to ask him for answers he might not be willing to give.

"We didn't catch them," he said.

Darby was surprised by the volunteered information.

"At least not by the time I knocked off to catch a few z's. I should call in and check the status of the situation."

He said the words, but made no move to implement them.

Darby found herself smiling. She wriggled her backside purposefully into his front, pleased by his immediate, undeniable reaction.

"I could make you some breakfast," she whispered.

He hummed, his hand leaving her hip and wandering over her abdomen, then down to tunnel into the V of her legs. The movement seemed so natural, so right, that her breath caught.

Oh, how wonderful it would be just to give herself over to the desire pulsing through her body like a powerful drug. To roll over and kiss John until her thirst for his mouth was somehow sated. Take his flesh into hers and make love to him until she could go no more.

John rubbed his stubble-dotted chin against her hair. "What will the girls say if they walk in and find us this way?"

"I don't know," she admitted. "But I know they won't be happy."

He began to roll away from her.

"No," she whispered, clamping her thighs around his hand and holding him close with her own hand. "Please. Just a few more minutes. This…this feels good."

She heard his thick swallow. "Darby—" his voice held warning "—if you don't let me get up this minute, we'll be doing more than just lying here together, I promise you."

Oh, how good that sounded.

She reluctantly released him and he rolled to the other side of the bed and got to his feet. She propped herself up on her elbows and watched him.

He still wore the same jeans and shirt from the day before. She realized she wore the same clothes, as well.

"Lindy was trying to talk to Erick on her two-way," she said quietly, not quite knowing why she'd told him but somehow needing to tell him. Needing to share the significant moment with someone who was growing in importance to her.

John's movements ceased, his gaze questioning.

She looked down at her stomach. "I was straightening up in here when I found the other radio. I changed the batteries and switched it on. I nearly hit the ceiling when I heard her."

John sat back down on the mattress as if no longer able to stand. "Good Lord."

Darby tried to even her breathing. "I know."

"That's why you were crying." He glanced over his shoulder at her. "Did you talk to her?"

She shook her head. "No. I found her where she was hiding in the closet and just held her. I...I didn't know what else to do."

John ran his hands through his hair several times. Then he reached out, resting a strong, long-fingered hand against her blanket-covered leg. She put her hand on top of it, filled with gratitude that he was there to help her shoulder the burden, act as a sympathetic ear.

He glanced at her. "Do you want me to try to talk to her?"

She shook her head. "I think she sees you as trying to take Erick's place, so I don't know if that's such a good idea."

Silence reigned as they sat there, individually considering the situation.

Darby squeezed his hand. "I'm going to take the girls to church this morning, then we're going to spend the afternoon at Jolie's painting eggs for Easter."

He nodded, leaving unsaid what he would be doing. He would be doing his job. And that included hunting down two very dangerous men.

She looked up to find him watching her carefully. "Will you be okay?" he asked.

She smiled. "Yeah. You?"

That got a grin from him.

She sighed. "Oh, yeah. I forgot. We're talking about the big ol' strong sheriff here. Of course you'll be fine."

"I take offense at the old part."

"I said ol', not old."

"We'll settle that later. I'll try to make it home for dinner. I'll call and let you know."

*Home.* How very right the word sounded to her coming from his handsome mouth.

He leaned across the bed, bringing that same mouth even with hers. She put a hand over her mouth, afraid she had morning breath. He grinned and moved her hand away. "Trust me, it can't be as bad as the goat's."

She laughed and he kissed her.

"Marry me, Darby," he whispered, his hazel eyes dark and somber as he rested his nose against hers.

She forced herself to stop smiling. "You know, I'm supposed to be scaring you away from the prospect of marrying me, not encouraging you."

"I think you should just give in now."

Longing to do just that filled her, thickened her blood. "A little smug, aren't you?"

"No," he said, shaking his head, their noses still touching. "Just hopeful."

Warmth, sure and strong, flooded Darby's limbs, making her feel like a teenager again experiencing her first crush. That that crush even then had been on the man gazing at her right now...well, she refused to see that as kismet. Too much had happened since then.

He moved away from her and toward the door, peeking out first to make sure the coast was clear.

Darby sank against the pillows, watching him, realizing that this time she hadn't given him an answer to his question. She wondered exactly what, if anything, that meant.

"Even Dusty is involved in the manhunt," Jolie said out of earshot of the twins and her foster child, Ellie.

They stood at the far counter in Jolie's bright and cheery kitchen, while the kids sat behind them on the other side of an island at a pine table. They'd returned home from Sunday church service two hours ago, had lunch, then used egg boiling as an excuse to chat quietly.

Darby glanced at Jolie. "Dusty is? You're kidding me?"

Her friend shook her head. "I guess these two fugitives are the real deal. The kind they make television films out of, you know? Every man in town wants in on the hunt." She slanted a gaze at Darby. "You know, there aren't too many opportunities for them to play hero here." She glanced away. "This is the first time since the big fire last year."

"You think that's why they're all doing it? To be heroes?" Darby shook her head. "I don't think that's why John is doing it. He wouldn't even know the definition of the word *hero*. He would say he's just doing his job."

"Dusty, too."

Darby paused from the business of mixing egg-coloring solutions in oversize juice glasses. "You don't think Dusty plans to blacken his other eye, do you? The one has just healed."

Jolie laughed. "I think he considered it after getting word that John had moved out to the farm. But I think that storm cloud has blown over. For now, anyway." She gave Darby a loaded look. "However, I wouldn't count on it not making a return if the two of you don't hurry up and tie the knot."

Darby nearly knocked over a vial of green dye.

Jolie homed in on her. "Don't tell me you're still refusing to marry him, Darby."

Darby glanced toward the twins, but amazingly

they seemed engaged in their own activities dragging wax crayons over hard-boiled eggs. This once she wished they had been paying attention.

Up to this point, she'd managed to put off her friend whenever she brought up the subject of the baby, or John, either finding an excuse to end their phone conversation or quickly changing the subject. She had the sinking sensation Jolie wasn't going to let her do the same now. She glanced to find her friend smiling in determination.

"Come on, Darby. The guy loves you. You have to know that," Jolie said quietly.

Darby suddenly found it difficult to swallow. "Do I?"

Jolie stopped drying the eggs she had taken from a pan of cool water. "Oh, my God, you don't know, do you."

Darby felt her cheeks redden, but lifted her chin just the same.

"Hmm, you know it wasn't so long ago that we had another conversation like this. Only, the man was Erick." Jolie crossed her arms and leaned against the counter.

Darby balked. "John and Erick are nothing alike. They may have been best friends, but two different men you couldn't find should you search the world over and back again."

Jolie's smile told Darby she had stepped right through the door she'd just cracked open.

"You're sneaky, you know that?"

Jolie shrugged. "A woman's gotta do what a woman's gotta do."

Darby turned her gaze to the window. Spring had kissed the grass with green, and fresh buds were popping out all over the oak tree. "Erick was the quintessential hotshot, you know? I think it stemmed from his being Dusty's younger brother. Or maybe the next in line in a family of firefighters, I don't know. But it always seemed to me that he was desperate to prove something." She frowned. "No, not desperate. He was driven. Or determined. Yes, that's the word. Determined. He wanted to be the best just because he didn't know any other way to be." She cleared her throat and recapped the vial she held. "I always felt I came in a distant second to that, you know? Even though he loved me fully. Was always gentle with me. As if he wanted to be the best in that department, too."

"And John?" Jolie asked.

Darby instantly smiled, her shoulders relaxing. "John is...well, John is just John," she said.

Jolie continued drying eggs. "Uh-huh," she encouraged.

"Oh, you know," Darby said, not certain she really wanted to get into John's many qualities for fear of what she might find herself.

"Uh-huh."

Ultimately Darby couldn't resist talking about the man who was on her mind day and night, even haunting her dreams. The man whose essence clung to her like a second skin. "John is just John. He doesn't need to prove anything to anyone. He does what he thinks is right straight out of the box, no second-guessing, but he's open-minded enough to admit it when he's wrong. He's sheriff not because anyone in his family was, but because the job needed to be filled and he thought he could fill it. So he hung up his firefighting cap and ran unopposed.''

''Uh-huh,'' Jolie said again.

Darby nudged her with her arm. ''Isn't that enough?''

''You said Erick was gentle with you, as if he needed to be the best in the bedroom, too.''

Darby gasped and gaped at her friend.

''Come on, Dar, both you and I know that's what you were talking about. It's only fair you give John his due.''

''I'm going to tell Dusty you're interested in other men's performances.''

''No, you won't. Because then you'd be revealing that I've told you about his he-man antics.''

Darby laughed so hard she couldn't see straight. ''Okay. You're right there.

''So...''

Darby shrugged, her skin growing hot just thinking about John's attentions. ''He's...passionate. Almost rough, but not quite. Not afraid to show me how he really feels. And what he seems to feel is this need to...possess me somehow. Chase everything else from my mind and my heart so there's room for only him.''

Jolie had grown quiet. ''And is it working?''

Darby was suddenly incapable of swallowing.

''I'll take that as a yes,'' Jolie said, her smile making a comeback. ''You know, Dar, I think it would be a good idea to put your ideas aside for a minute and take a closer look at the man independent of everything going on."

Darby's free hand instantly sought and found her rounded belly. "Kind of hard to overlook a baby, Jol."

"I didn't say to overlook it. I said to take a peek at the larger picture."

"I am," Darby whispered.

"Are you?"

There was a ruckus at the table behind them. "That's mine!" Erin cried. "Give it back!"

Darby turned to watch Erin practically launch herself at Lindy.

"Is not!" Lindy yelled back. "You were done with it, so I started using it, and that's the only reason you want it back."

Darby picked up the three cups of dye solution and walked to the table, placing them on the thick sheets of newspaper Jolie had spread to protect the table the same way plastic aprons protected the girls. "That's enough. Erin, you can use the crayon again when Lindy's done with it." She wiped her hands on her own cloth apron and bent to Ellie. "Let's see what you've done, El."

The little girl gladly held up her egg.

"Ooooh, that's pretty," she said of the dots and slashes the five-year-old had made.

She sat down next to Erin while Jolie took a chair next to Lindy. They both looked through the eggs waiting to be dyed.

Darby ran her fingertips over a particularly skillful

depiction of the holiday. "Oh, Erin. This is wonderful. Jesus rising. Very good."

Lindy made a face. "That's not Jesus. It's Daddy."

Darby nearly choked on her own saliva as she stared at the girl she'd spent much of the night holding, then looked at Jolie who appeared just as shocked as she felt.

The two-way radio, the holiday, John's presence in their lives—it all came together to paint a clearer picture of what was going on in her daughter's young mind.

And left Darby even more clueless about what to do about it.

## Chapter Twelve

Front-porch sitting. John couldn't remember a time when he'd enjoyed it more. Or enjoyed it at all. Of course, his trailer didn't even have a front porch. But as a kid, he used to hate being on the porch of his family's house because it usually meant either his mother had booted everyone out so she could clean or watch one of her soap operas, or one of his brothers had locked him out because he, the brother, had had a girlfriend inside and John wouldn't leave them be.

Then, of course, there was the whole old fogey factor. Whenever he got a call from anyone over sixty with a front porch, it was more than likely that that's where he'd find them. Weather permitting. It was also the reason why so many of them got into trouble, or earned a reputation for being nosy. You had a bird's-eye view of the world sitting out here. But sitting next to Darby on the front porch of her hundred-year-old farmhouse, his stomach full of the wonderful dinner she'd made, the girls chasing the dandelion fluff that floated on the light breeze as the sun set behind them, made him feel...well, damn good. A state that was especially notable since neither he nor his men had had any luck recapturing the escaped prisoners.

It had been more than thirty-six hours since their escape and still not a single lead. No truck drivers had come forward with stories of any strange hitch-hikers. No unusual sightings. No sign of them at all, either together or apart. It was as if they'd knocked Ed over the head, taken his gun and simply disappeared. Which didn't make the U.S. Marshal's Service happy with John or his office. And that was saying nothing about what the blow had done to his ego.

That is, until he pulled into the gravel drive leading to Darby's house and felt all of that melt away. Darby standing in the doorway waiting for him erased all the bad and filled him with nothing but good.

He snaked his hand along the back of the swing, brushing Darby's shoulders.

Maybe he'd have to give his whole theory on marriage and parenthood a fresh review. While he and the twins still had a way to go before they made it through the rough patch they were in, he was confident that they would. And just knowing Darby was here, waiting for him to come home, well, definitely had its benefits. Even if he hadn't found a way to sneak into her bed for good. Yet.

He curved a hand around her shoulder and she

smiled at him. "You know, you haven't even taken me out on a proper date yet."

John's eyes widened, and he wondered if he'd jumped to conclusions about the benefits of porch sitting. "Pardon me?"

Darby snuggled closer to his side. "I don't know. I was just thinking about how...secret everything has been between us."

He gazed down at her, the setting sun kissing her brown curls with touches of auburn. "Darby, everyone knows I'm living out here now. They don't know the details, but they know that much. And as for the baby..."

She waved her hand. "I'm not talking about that. I'm talking about us." She rubbed her cheek against his denim shirtfront. "You aren't ashamed of me, are you, John?"

"What?" he fairly croaked.

Now where in hell would she get an idea like that?

She shrugged, then tucked her legs under her. "Do you realize we've never actually been out? You know, on a date date."

He grimaced. "Are you talking about dinner? A movie? That kind of thing?"

She nodded. "Yes. Exactly that kind of thing."

He stroked her cheek with his other hand. "If you want to go out, all you have to do is ask, Darby."

She laughed and smacked at his hand. "That's not what I mean and you know it." She straightened and he was forced to move his hand to the swing back where it had started out. "I mean this whole... courtship thing has been a little backward."

"Courtship?"

"Yes, courtship. I mean, it's supposed to work the other way. First the guy asks a girl for a date. Then they go out on another. Then maybe by the third or the fourth date, maybe they kiss."

"By then she had better be doing a whole lot more than kissing," he grumbled.

She swatted at him again and he ducked. "Will you stop? You know what I mean."

He leaned back and crossed his feet at the ankles. "Yeah, I know what you mean." He ran his hands through his hair. "There was a time when I felt everything was moving a little too fast myself."

"But you don't feel that way now?"

He shook his head and grinned. "No."

She made a face and sat back again. He automatically put his hand back where he felt it belonged and started kneading her shoulder.

"Do you really think I'm ashamed of you?" he asked quietly, the possibility bothering him.

"No. It's just...I don't know. Maybe doing things normal couples do will help me feel somehow more..."

"Normal?"

She laughed. "Sounds stupid, doesn't it?"

He shook his head. "Not at all." He glanced at the girls. They had abandoned the dandelion fluff and were now chasing the goat around the yard. "So when can you get a sitter for the night?" he asked.

"For the whole night?"

He watched a light blush creep over her smooth cheeks, then she looked away.

"That's not being normal," she whispered.

He rubbed his hand up and down her back, absorbing her shiver. "Normal is what we make it, Darby." He leaned toward her and nibbled on the tip of her ear just as he'd learned she liked it. "So what do you say?"

"Is tomorrow soon enough?" she asked.

He felt her hot body next to his and was filled with the urge to tug her into his lap. "I was hoping you'd say tonight."

She licked her lips, a combination nervous/hungry move that made him want to kiss away her fears. "You know, you haven't asked me to marry you yet tonight," she said quietly.

He grinned, his gaze flicking over her face. "That's because I'm still waiting for an answer from this morning."

She turned back to face the girls, her smile decidedly mischievous, her body language undeniably sexy. And John wanted her more in that one minute than he'd ever wanted her before.

The only problem was, he didn't think he was going to have her. At least not tonight, anyway.

John's parents' house was not exactly what Darby had in mind when she suggested she and John go out, but it was what she got the following night. As John pulled up to the neat, two-story structure a couple of blocks from downtown Old Orchard on a picturesque, tree-lined street, she suddenly felt nauseous.

Sure, she knew the Sparks family. It was difficult not to, what with eight kids terrorizing the town. But she'd never been to their house before. And she'd never actually met Walter and Edith Sparks, John's parents.

John turned off the ignition and stared at the quiet house along with her. "They're probably all peeking through the sheers at us."

"All?" she practically croaked.

He grimaced and nodded toward the cars in the driveway and lining the street. "I think every last one of my brothers and sisters is here. Except for Julie. She lives in Chicago. Although I wouldn't be surprised if Mom had her flown in especially for the occasion."

Darby stared at him in shock. There hadn't been that many people at her graduation. "How long have you had this planned?"

"A whole two hours." He rubbed his face with both hands, revealing his own anxiety. "Mom called earlier, said if I didn't bring you by for dinner tonight, she and my sisters were going to pay you a visit tomorrow." He shrugged so helplessly that Darby almost smiled. "I figured this way I could at least run interference."

She nodded. It was well-known that the Sparks family was very reactionary. Something happened, they were the first on the scene. She supposed it went hand in hand with being accustomed to dealing with crises. You didn't have a family that big without knowing how to handle whatever came your way.

She noticed she had a death grip on the door handle and forced herself to release it. "What...what have you told them? You know, about us?"

"Nothing."

She lifted her brows.

"Nothing they didn't already know from the grapevine. I just did a lot of nodding when I dropped by a couple of days after you told me about the baby." He turned so that he was facing her. "Look, Darby, if you don't want to do this, I understand. Hell, I'd prefer a nice night out at Manny's Steakhouse down on Main to this myself, but I was railroaded into it. Say the word, though, and I'll pull away from this curb and head to Manny's."

She stared into his honest hazel eyes and knew he would do just that. She glanced back at the house and saw one of the sheers covering the windows flutter. If they left now, she wondered if she'd ever be able to live it down. She absently rubbed her belly. These people were to be her child's extended family. Loving aunts and uncles. Doting grandparents. Certainly she couldn't deny them or her child that.

She pulled in a deep breath and held it for a few seconds before releasing it. "Okay. Let's go."

"Are you..."

But Darby was already halfway out of the car. She figured if she didn't take the initiative, they'd likely sit in the Jeep all night watching the sheers flutter. She closed the car door and straightened her skirt, trying to guess what she was in for and failing miserably. As an only child, she was frightfully uneducated about large families. And she was afraid she was going to be given a crash course.

"Uncle Sparky!" Four kids barreled from the front of the house and made a beeline for John. She thought of the twins; they were at her mother's house and she was glad that at least she didn't have *them* to worry about. All she needed was Lindy or Erin proclaiming, in front of John's family, that their daddy was coming back. No, she had enough to cope with as it was.

A slender woman stepped onto the front porch, followed by four boys of various sizes, and then what seemed like the entire Old Orchard Women's Club. The slender woman came down the stairs, then the sidewalk. "Hi, John." She looked at Darby and smiled, extending her hand. "Hi, Darby. It's nice to meet you. I mean face-to-face. I'm Bonnie. John's brother Ben's wife. And these guys are our four monsters."

Darby cleared her throat. "Nice to meet you...all."

"I'm on my way to drop the kids off at their cousin's now." Her expression became sympathetic. "Between you and me, I think the house is full enough already."

John stuffed his hands into his jeans pockets and grimaced. "Yeah, amazing what Mom can do in two hours, isn't it?"

Bonnie leaned in closer to John. "Just make sure they don't scare her off, John. From what I hear, this one's a keeper."

She smiled at Darby, then gathered her four boys and headed for one of the minivans parked at the curb.

As she smiled at the remainder of John's family, Darby threw him a glance. "Bring many women home, do you?"

John's own grin looked forced and almost painful. "Nope. You're the first."

Darby felt something warm and thick spread through her chest. Something that made standing through the next fifteen minutes of introductions easier, somehow. John had never brought a woman home? Well, no wonder they were all curious about her.

Just as she was curious about all of them.

She'd always wondered about large families. Having grown up on a steady diet of *The Brady Bunch* and *The Partridge Family,* she'd thought it would be nice to have a houseful of people connected in such a close way. And it was nice to see she wasn't wrong. As they all settled around the huge dining-room table, she thought the laughter of twenty people, given their different timbres and individual qualities, was wonderfully unique and incredibly moving. Not to mention noisy. She couldn't hear herself think, much less have time to worry about how she looked.

Darby draped her napkin across her lap, slanting a gaze toward the head of the table and John's father, Walter. He hadn't said much since she'd come in. Merely nodded when they were introduced, then disappeared into the woodwork again. John's mother, Edith, on the other hand, seemed all smiles and boundless energy, scoffing at the hand Darby offered and hugging her so tightly Darby could barely breathe. One minute Edith was in front of her, chattering away about how happy she was that John was finally settling down, the next she was carrying some sort of heaping dish or other from the kitchen. The frenzied activity was enough to make Darby dizzy.

John reached over and took her hand under the table, giving her fingers a gentle squeeze. She gazed at him gratefully, his touch providing the grounding she needed right that moment.

''So when's the baby due?''

''Are you going to have a traditional wedding?''

''Don't you have twin girls? We can't wait to meet them.''

''How did you manage to hook the last Sparks bachelor?''

The questions came one after another, sometimes on top of each other. Darby managed to smile her way through most of them, allowing John to answer the more iffy ones. She leaned closer to him. ''You told them we were getting married?'' she whispered.

He glanced at her. ''I told them I asked you to marry me. There's a difference.'' He grinned. ''Of course they automatically assumed you would accept.''

She could certainly understand why. Any woman would be insane to reject a man like John Sparks. As it was, Darby was having a hard enough time.

''Let's see the ring,'' another of John's sisters-in-law said from across the table.

Darby froze. She had hidden her left hand under the table at the first question about her and John's wedding date. The same hand John held.

After a long, awkward moment John cleared his throat. ''I, um, haven't exactly bought her a ring yet.''

The room went silent. For the first time Darby

heard a grandfather clock ticking somewhere. But before she could isolate where, the room erupted into a current of indignant protests from the women and sympathetic glances at John from the men.

"John!" his mother's voice rose above everyone else's. "I thought I raised you better than that."

His father made a sound from the other end of the table. "Better he should save his money to support all those kids."

Darby nearly choked on the water she was drinking.

"Oh, don't be ridiculous," Edith Sparks said. "Who should know better than us that you always have a way of finding money. An engagement ring is a once-in-a-lifetime gift."

Darby raised her right hand to prevent further argument. "Actually..." she said over the din. Silence immediately settled over the table. She saw all the expectant faces and regretted opening her mouth. "John has presented me with a ring. A beautiful ring."

A couple of the women nodded in anticipation.

"Is it being sized?" one asked, unable to stand the suspense.

"You didn't like it. You took it back for another," someone else offered up before Darby could respond to the first.

"No, I love it," she said with a smile, squeezing John's hand with hers under the table.

John put his napkin on his plate. "You see, Darby has yet to accept my proposal."

Eyebrows shot up, mouths dropped open, and the

sound of someone's silverware clattering to their plate echoed through the room.

"Oh," a sister-in-law said.

John's father chuckled. "Smart woman."

"So how about those Indians?" John's older brother Ben asked. "The season's started and they're looking strong. World Series, here we come."

John was wound up tighter than a ball of wire when he finally spirited Darby out his parents' front door sometime after nine. They might have left sooner, but Darby had asked his mother for the recipe of one of the dishes she'd made that night and had actually seemed to enjoy a conversation she got into with his older sister, Josephine.

Him? He'd been ready to bolt for the door the instant his father made the crack about his saving his money.

He held the door to the Jeep open for Darby, then rounded the vehicle and climbed in the other side.

"Well, that wasn't as bad as I thought it would be," Darby said, waving at the family members who stood on the front porch.

"Easy for you to say. I think that qualifies for one of the worst nights of my life."

Darby laughed quietly and he pulled from the curb, not even glancing back at his family, much less acknowledging them with a wave.

She scooted closer to him and put her hand on his leg. "The night's not over yet, Sheriff," she whispered.

Everything that had happened over the past three

hours shot out of John's head, as heat, sure and swift, raced to his groin.

Darby sighed. "It must have been great growing up in a big family," she said, a faraway look on her face. "Always something going on. Always someone to talk to."

"Always a line to go to the bathroom. Never enough food in the fridge." John glanced at her. "Don't romanticize my family, Darby. They'll make you regret it."

"I doubt that."

He put his hand over hers where it lay on his thigh and inched it upward ever so slightly. She glanced at him and smiled.

"Your dad seemed a little off-putting."

He grimaced. "That's Dad for you. If he's not condemning the pope for outlawing birth control, he's cursing Mom's fertility."

He felt her gaze on him and inwardly winced, wondering if he'd revealed a bit too much.

"But he loves you all. You know that, don't you?" she asked quietly.

He shrugged. "I suppose."

She squeezed his leg. "I know. I saw the looks he gave all of you throughout dinner. The pride that beamed from his face. The love."

"Maybe he had indigestion."

Darby lay her head back against the headrest, voluntarily inching her hand up a little farther. John nearly groaned, suppressing the desire to slide down in his seat so that her hand would be exactly where he wanted it.

"I'm sorry about that."

He looked at her in the light from the streetlamps they passed. "Sorry about what?"

"I don't know. Your brothers must have given you quite a ribbing when we told them we weren't engaged."

"Yet," he corrected, then grinned. "Actually I got a few congratulations, if you can believe it."

She gaped at him.

"Ben said he thought it was the first time in Old Orchard history that a guy knocked a woman up and a shotgun wedding didn't follow the next day."

"Must be a guy thing."

"Yeah."

He'd had something in mind all night, and it had driven him crazy just thinking about it. Whenever things were at their worst throughout the night— which for him was almost every moment—he'd remember where he planned to take Darby and would find himself grinning stupidly. His brothers had teased him, telling him that he was in love. He hadn't worked that part out yet, but he did know he was definitely in lust. And that he couldn't seem to get his fill of the sexy woman next to him.

He pulled onto a dark gravel road.

"John?" Darby asked, looking around. "Where are you taking me?"

"Where do you think I'm taking you?"

She squinted through the window, the yellow light from the dash casting shadows against her face. "I think you're taking me to Lovers' Leap." She sat back. "Not planning on jumping, are you?"

"The story about that lovelorn girl jumping from the cliff in the 1950s is a myth."

"It's documented fact."

"Oh, really? Where?"

"All the newspapers at the time wrote about it."

"No. All the newspapers wrote about was the mystery surrounding the rumor. No body was ever found."

He caught her smile as she said, "If you were hoping to make this a romantic outing, I think you're failing."

He chuckled as he pulled to a stop at an area just short of the cliff where the trees gave way, offering a breathtaking view of the lights of the town some hundred yards down and half a mile west of the cliff. Before he could switch off the ignition, Darby was cuddling up to his side.

"Come up here often, Sheriff Sparks?"

His breath caught in his throat as her hand finally found the part begging for her attention for the past fifteen minutes. "All the time," he said roughly. "I bring all my dates here."

She reached for and found the release for his seat and it slid all the way back. She took advantage of the space and straddled him. "Liar."

He grinned, his arousal growing by the second. "Yeah, well, that may be the case. But obviously you're an old pro at this."

She leaned forward and kissed him. "Maybe." She ran the tip of her tongue across his bottom lip. "Wanna see what I know?"

Oh, boy, *did* he.

Things got hot and heavy very fast, with John claiming her mouth with a hunger that surprised even him, his hands finding their way up her cotton shirt and to her breasts, plucking at her gloriously engorged nipples. Darby shifted, tugging up the hem of her skirt so that he could gain closer contact. John groaned when he realized all that separated them were his jeans and her cotton panties.

He jerked his leg when she ground her hips, bumping his knee on the dash. He cursed and continued his assault on her hot, delectable mouth. Tasting wine there. And chocolate-mousse. And one-hundred-percent-needy Darby.

When he pushed her back slightly to gain access to her breasts, she knocked her head on the ceiling. Her soft yelp of pain was followed by a deep moan as he fastened his lips around a stiff crest, pulling a nipple deep into his mouth and swirling his tongue around it.

He slid down farther in the seat, his hips bucking up against her as he fumbled for his fly. This time both knees jammed against the dash.

Darby giggled. ''You know, there's this perfectly empty house, with a perfectly big, soft bed waiting for us not ten minutes from here.''

He growled deep in his throat. ''I don't think I can wait that long.''

She pushed his hand out of the way and unfastened his fly. ''Good. Because neither can I.''

A light tapping of something solid against the window next to them sent John jackknifing into a sitting position, knocking Darby's head against the ceiling again. Darby scrambled to pull her top down even as John used her skirt to cover...certain strategic areas.

He pressed the button to open the window a couple of inches.

"John? Is that you in there?"

John cursed under his breath as he realized who it was. A flashlight beam hit him square in the eyes even as guessed he'd never be able to live this one down. "Turn that damn thing off, Cole," he told the deputy sheriff.

"Oh. Sorry." Cole fumbled to do just that, then tipped his head to Darby. "Evening Ms. Conrad."

"Hi, Cole," she said, and John heard the laughter in her voice.

"Cole, what do you want?" John asked impatiently.

The deputy stood up straight. "Well, John, I don't think I have to tell you this, but, um, public display of affection to a certain degree is illegal in these parts." John could see him fighting a grin. "Would you like me to lend you my code book? Maybe you need to brush up."

"And maybe I need to sock you in the jaw."

Cole's grin didn't budge. "That, sir, would get you into even more trouble than you're in now."

"Yeah, but it would be worth it."

Cole stepped back, as if suddenly uncertain of John's intention. "I'm going to have to ask you to move on, Sheriff."

"Fine. Just fine."

"Now."

"I'll get out of here just as soon as you go back to your car, deputy."

"As you wish."

Ah, if life were only that simple. If it were, Cole would have disappeared altogether.

John pushed the button to close the window, then exhaled, his condition dampened not at all by the interruption. Not when he had Darby flush up against his erection, her panties damp and hot.

" I think we'd better do as the deputy says," he said.

"Yes. I was thinking the same thing."

She said the words, but didn't move.

"Darby, if you don't want Cole to have a front-row seat to a live sex show, then I'd suggest you, um, move to the other seat."

She laughed, then kissed him lingeringly. "How fast do you think you can get us home?"

He groaned, loving the feel of her tongue in his mouth, hearing her quickened breathing in his ears, feeling her softness pressing against his hardness. "Blink, baby, and we'll be there."

## Chapter Thirteen

John burrowed deeply under the covers, reaching for the woman who eluded him at every turn. Finally his fingers found her and he hauled her to him so that her back rested against his front. He grinned and made a sound deep in his throat.

"John?"

"Hmm?" John slowly came to realize it wasn't a dream, but reality. Darby was in his arms. And that was exactly where he intended to keep her. Forever. Or at least for the next few minutes or so.

"John?" her whispered voice became more insistent and she grabbed at his hands.

"What?" This time John popped open an eye. And when he did, he wished he hadn't.

Standing on Darby's side of the bed were two unhappy-looking little girls.

"You've been very bad," Erin said, shaking a finger at both of them. "Very, very bad."

John released Darby more out of fear than her struggle to free herself.

What were the twins doing there? Not just in the bedroom, but at the house at all? They were supposed to be at Darby's mother's house until later. Much later. He squinted at the clock. It was only 7:00 a.m.

"Sorry." Adelia Parker's voice came from the open bedroom door. "I got called into work and had to bring the girls home now."

This time John scrambled to sit up, fighting Darby for the sheet she was using to cover herself.

Suddenly Darby's bedroom had turned into Grand Central Station at rush hour.

"Mom." Erin tugged on the sheet, threatening to pull it from both of them as she vied for Darby's attention.

"In a minute," Darby said, looking at her daughter. Then she closed her eyes and took a deep breath. "Mother, would you please take the girls downstairs so I can get dressed?"

If John wasn't mistaken, Adelia Parker was fighting a smile. "Okay. But I only have five minutes."

Darby nodded. "Five minutes. That's enough. Plenty."

No one made a move.

"Go," Darby said in a steely voice.

The twins scrambled from the room, leaving John and Darby staring at the closed door.

"I can't believe that just happened," she whispered.

John ran his hand through his hair several times, trying to get a handle on the situation. "Yeah, it's a first for me, too."

He looked at her. God, she was beautiful. Her brown hair curled around her face in soft waves, her cheeks were filled with color, her green eyes danced with amusement.

"So...do I dare take up where I left off?" he asked, hiking a brow and allowing his gaze to skim her body.

Darby dropped the sheet so that it puddled around her waist, leaving her marvelous breasts bare.

John groaned and tackled her back down to the pillows, nuzzling her neck with his morning stubble.

"Mom? Are you done yet?" a small, irritated voice came through the closed door.

John looked at Darby. "Not nearly," she whispered.

He smoothed her hair back from her face repeatedly, then kissed her. "A rain check?"

She smiled. "Yes." She squeezed his shoulders. "But next time we get a different baby-sitter."

"You know, the girls should get used to having him around," Adelia told Darby a few minutes later. They were standing by the counter in the kitchen. "And not just in the guest bedroom."

Darby looked at her mother, trying to guess at her motives. It seemed everyone as of late was trying to push her into John's arms. Not that it took all that much effort anymore. On a physical level, she was more than willing to admit there was something special between them and had stopped fighting. The rest was what remained blurry.

"Is that the real reason for the early-morning visit?" she asked her mother quietly.

"No," Adelia looked affronted. "But as long as I'm here, I thought I should say something."

Darby grimaced and glanced at the clock. "I thought you only had five minutes."

"I can squeeze out a few more." Adelia leaned against the counter, sipping the coffee she'd made while Darby had dressed.

"I bet you can."

Her mother glanced to where the girls were pouting into their cereal bowls. She kept her voice low. "You know, they're not very happy about John being around."

Just then, Darby really didn't care what the girls were or were not happy about. She'd just about exhausted her patience with the girls and their animosity toward John. A good, long talk was overdue. And just as soon as John left for the office, and her mother for work, she and the twins were going one-on-two.

That moment came quickly. Her mother gave up trying to engage Darby in any conversation concerning her new living arrangements, and John practically shot through the kitchen in his crisp sheriff's uniform, pausing for a quick kiss to Darby's cheek and a wave to the girls, who reacted with fierce scowls.

Finally Darby was alone with the twins, who returned to pouting into their cereal bowls.

Darby crossed her arms, waiting for one or the

other to look up at her. Not surprisingly, Erin was the first.

Darby raised a brow, trying not to tap her foot. "So what do you have to say for yourselves?"

"Us?" Erin said incredulously. "You were the one being bad."

Darby picked up the bowls and placed them in the sink, then sat down in the chair across from them. "How, exactly, was I being bad?"

"You were sleeping with…with…"

"The man I love," she said.

Darby caught her breath. But the instant the words came out of her mouth, she felt the rightness of them. Warmth and a thrill of excitement raced over her skin, making her feel whole, somehow. And making her feel better equipped to deal with two very nosy, meddling little girls.

"You love Daddy," Erin said.

Darby cleared her throat. She hadn't intended to have the conversation concerning their father right now, but seeing as it likely tied into everything else that was going on around the house recently, she figured she had better face it head-on.

"Yes, Erin, I did love your daddy. Very much. And he loved all of us."

She had both twins' attention now.

She recrossed her legs and straightened her robe. "Do you remember the talk we had after Daddy's accident?"

They nodded in unison.

"How I said that Daddy had gone to heaven, and that while he'll always be with us here—" she covered her heart with her hand ''—physically he's gone forever?''

Clearly they remembered.

Darby attempted to rein in her own emotions, not wanting to come down too hard on them where their father was concerned. Reminding herself that the girls had lost a parent. ''It's very difficult to let Daddy go. I know that.'' Her voice was quiet, steady. ''But you have to understand that no matter what you think has happened…he's not coming back.''

Tears shone in Lindy's eyes, and all the starch drained out of Darby.

''Told you so,'' Erin said, glaring at her sister.

Okay, so that meant only Lindy held tightly to the belief that her father would return.

Darby focused her gaze on Erin. ''You and I need to talk about your attitude toward John. But for now I want you to go upstairs.''

''Why?''

''Because I said so.'' Darby cringed. She'd sworn she'd never use those words on her own children. Lord knows she'd heard them often enough from her own mother while growing up. That now should serve as the time she would understand why made her grimace. ''And I want you to stay up there until I call you back down.''

''But—''

''No buts. Go.''

Erin wriggled, but didn't get up.

''Now.''

Finally Erin budged from her chair and stomped from the room as if Darby was the worst parent in the world. And that was okay, Darby realized. For the past year, in her efforts to help the girls through their grief, she feared she had tried to be their best friend, instead of their mother. It was long past time she stretched her parenting muscles.

Lindy sat with her chin tucked into her tiny chest, the tears that had been sparkling in her eyes now gliding down her cheeks. As soon as Darby heard Erin slam her bedroom door upstairs, she reached for Lindy. "Come here," she said, and pulled her onto her lap. With the sleeve of her robe she wiped the moisture from her daughter's cheeks only to watch as even more tears fell.

She ducked her head to try to catch Lindy's gaze. "Lindy, look at me."

The girl blinked her brown eyes and did as Darby asked.

"I know you thought Daddy spoke to you on your radio—"

"He did."

Lindy's quivering chin nearly did Darby in. She took a deep breath and held her daughter closer. "Okay. Let's say for the sake of argument that he did speak to you." She smoothed her hair back from her face and fought to keep her gaze from straying. "Do you think it could have been to say goodbye?"

Lindy didn't respond.

"Your daddy loved you—you know that, don't you? He loved both you and Erin more than anything in the whole wide world."

"And…you." Lindy's voice broke.

Darby smiled and leaned her chin against her

daughter's sweet-smelling head. "Yes. Me, too." She rocked the six-year-old slightly. "I think it's important for you to know that it wasn't anything you did. Daddy didn't leave because he was mad at you. Or me. Or Erin. It's just that God needed your daddy more than we did." She pressed a kiss to her hair. "And he's not coming back, sweetie."

"But he is," Lindy whispered. "He is."

Darby pulled back and looked her in the face.

"He's coming back because Jesus came back," the little girl said. "And if he can come back, why can't Daddy?"

Oh, dear. "Sweetheart, Jesus rose from the dead. That much is right. But then he went up to heaven to join his father, God. Just like your daddy did."

"But…"

Darby noticed that this *but* was a little hesitant, Lindy a little less sure of herself.

"He's not coming back, sweet pea. He's just not."

Her daughter started crying again, softly.

Darby merely sat there holding Lindy and slightly rocking her as the child's words and the meaning behind them sank in.

"Sometimes the world works in mysterious ways, Lindy," she said at last. "Sometimes what happens isn't fair. Other times wonderful things happen, too."

The girl's quiet sobs began to subside.

Darby smiled as she again used the sleeve of her robe to dry the tears, then reached for a paper napkin on the table to get Lindy to blow her nose. "You know, sometimes things have to happen, things that we don't understand, to nudge us down the paths that are mapped out for us.''

"Like destiny?" Lindy asked, her curiosity returning, which was a good sign. A good sign indeed.

"Yes. Very much like destiny."

Her daughter nodded and her thoughts seemed to turn inward, though she gave no indication that she was ready to get down off Darby's lap. So Darby remained where she was.

Then Lindy's eyes met Darby's. "Do you think Daddy sent Uncle Sparky to you and us?"

Darby caught her breath. Just when she thought she had the wending workings of her daughter's mind figured out, she'd fling a zinger like that at her, catching her completely off guard.

Only this zinger felt somehow…right.

She smiled at Lindy, then pressed her lips to her forehead. "You know, he just might have."

John stood staring at his office wall. A map of the tri-state area stretched across it, bearing pins of the main routes, secondary routes, the Maumee River and the outlying areas where the two escapees could lie low until the search ground down. He ran his hand through his hair, then scratched his head. Only a handful of calls had come in on possible sightings. All of them had been explained away. A paperboy delivering his papers much later than he should have, raising the suspicions of an elderly neighbor who didn't subscribe. A farmer searching for his wayward cow. And, of course, there were the calls from Elva Mollenkopf reporting odd incidents—and to her basically everything that happened in the town was odd. ''Old Jake is acting preoccupied. You think maybe the fugitives are hiding in the basement of his store?'' Or John's personal favorite, ''That Penelope Moon has always been strange. It would be just like her to take in the fugitives in the name of human rights. A kind of New Age underground railroad.''

John snatched up the phone and began dialing Darby's number. It was midafternoon and he hadn't talked to her since leaving this morning. This morning…

He misdialed, then pressed the disconnect button and held it.

Having been raised in such a large family, very few things were capable of embarrassing him. But waking up with disapproving six-year-olds staring at him as he lay in bed with their mother still made him cringe.

Over the past week he'd tried everything to get the girls to come around. And he'd succeeded to a degree. Away from Darby, the three of them seemed to have resumed their preproposal relationship. He rough-housed with them, drank tea out of teensy china cups and answered myriad questions on his job as sheriff.

But put him and Darby in the same room—much less the same bed, and the twins clammed up and glared at them as if they were doing something unforgivable.

And perhaps in their young eyes, he and Darby were doing something unforgivable. He couldn't begin to imagine losing one of his parents when he was their age. What pain they must have gone through, having their safe little world with two doting parents torn asunder.

Then, on the heels of that, to have their mother become intimately involved with a man they had known their entire lives as Uncle Sparky...

Poor Darby. While he could escape to work, she was left alone to deal with the two headstrong girls. He released the disconnect button and began dialing again. He was on the last number when something on the map caught his gaze. Receiver still in hand, he leaned back and looked at Ed, who, bandage firmly in place, was at the front desk, eating something.

"Ed? Has anyone checked out the Jenkins place?"

Mouth full, Ed turned his head toward him, his brow creased in thought. He swallowed. "Can't say as I know," he admitted. "Why?"

John slowly replaced the receiver.

Why indeed? It didn't make much sense for the fugitives to return to a house that had been nothing but a random stop on the way to their destination. Then again, no one had ever quite determined what the fugitives' ultimate destination had been. Why stop in Old Orchard at all? Why not continue on? Or why not bypass the town altogether?

He walked to the map and traced a line from the sheriff's office to Old Violet Jenkins's place. Once outside town, there would have been no one at home in any of the neighboring farms to see them, because the owners would have been away at work.

His gaze stopped at one farm in particular. Darby's farm. He smiled. He could always head over there for a quick...hello while checking out the Jenkins place.

He picked up his hat, checked his revolver and headed for the door.

"Ed, I'm going out there."

The older man wiped his mouth with a paper napkin. "You want me to call for backup?"

John hesitated near the door. "No. I'm probably on a wild-goose chase." He opened the door. "I'll give you a call when I get there."


John drove up Violet Jenkins's neatly paved driveway. The flowers she was known for were in full bloom when others' flowers had yet to break the surface. He glanced at the daffodils, multicolored tulips and lilac bushes that needed a little trimming hugging the front of the single-story white house. Violet had lived here with her husband for some forty years before Jasper died five years ago. They'd never had children. Whether it was by choice or because they'd been unable to, nobody knew for sure. The couple had kept pretty much to themselves, with Jasper commuting to the next town for his job as comptroller for the canning factory there. They'd attended church services in town, went to all the town events, were friendly and unassuming, but Violet appeared to prefer her garden to people. Seemed fitting, then, that her dead body was found slumped over her tulip bed six months ago, her gloved hands still buried in the soil.

John coasted to a stop, then switched off the ignition. The house didn't look any different than it had more than a week ago when he'd first apprehended Lyle and Ted Smythe. He'd been on a routine drivearound at the time, the Jenkins house a frequent stop because it was empty, and because of the rumors still circulating about what Violet had done with her husband's life insurance money. She'd never deposited it in her bank account. John stepped toward the side door. He preferred to think she gave the funds to charity. Others, however, were convinced she'd stashed it inside the house somewhere, sparking the interest of several local treasure hunters. He couldn't count the number of people he'd had to chase off in the weeks after Violet's death.

Things had been quiet lately, though. At least until the two fugitives had come to town.

John reached out and tried the doorknob. Locked. As it should be. He glanced through the window, saw nothing out of the ordinary inside and started toward the back of the house.

Lyle and Ted Smythe were probably long gone, Old Orchard nothing but a bitter memory for them. He rubbed the back of his neck and glanced at his watch. He wondered what Darby was doing. And whether or not she'd welcome a surprise visit.

He rounded the corner of the house and found out the hard way that his instincts had been right. The fugitives had, indeed, returned there.

If the whack to the back of the head wasn't proof enough, watching the two fugitives, still in sheriff's office jumpsuits, running away from him as he lay there trying to shake the bells ringing through his head definitely was.

Then he realized in which direction the fugitives were running.

"Damn."

John tried to scramble to his feet, but he fell back again and his world went black.

"Erin, don't feed Billy your chocolate-chip cookie—he'll get sick," Darby called from her side of the barn. It was midafternoon and they were nearly done with their chores. Which was more than okay with Darby, because it meant she was that much closer to the time she'd see John again.

Erin immediately put her hand behind her back and gave Darby a smile that was all innocence and sunshine. "What, Mommy? I wasn't feeding Billy anything."

Darby rolled her eyes and spread fresh straw in Lily the Llama's stall. The animal had been a neighbor's idea of a unique pet for his wife. Only his wife hadn't wanted the animal, or any animal for that matter, and within a week Darby found herself with a new addition to The Promised Land farm, along with a healthy donation to see to the animal's upkeep. Which was more than she got with most of the animals. Usually they were left either in a box or tied to her side door with no note. Although, given the size of the town, it wasn't difficult to find out who had left what.

Darby sidestepped the llama as the animal hoofed her way in to check out her clean digs. Following on Lily's footsteps was the runt of the barn cat's latest litter, making a nest in a corner of the stall, then curling up in it and going to sleep. Lily nosed the feline, then made a sound that conveyed to Darby a llama's version of a thumbs-up. Considering the interesting mix of animals, it wasn't all that unusual for different breeds to cozy up to each other. Darby smiled. This match was as unusual as it got.

"Happy you approve," she said, patting Lily's nose.

She backed out of the stall, taking her rake with her, one eye on the girls at the opposite end of the barn.

Lindy seemed to be adjusting well after their talk that morning, while her talk with Erin about her rudeness to John seemed to have fallen on deaf ears. Just when, she wondered, had Erin gotten so stubborn? She blew her hair from her brow and watched Erin snatch something out of Lindy's hand. Lindy gave chase and both girls ran outside the barn.

"Don't go where I can't see you," Darby said automatically.

Neither responded. She sighed and returned to her chores. All that was left was to check the hay bales for dampness and peek in on the new piglet.

After determining that the bales were fine, she stopped outside the indoor portion of the pen Arnold—named such by the girls who didn't understand the sex argument—and her own six piglets called home and crossed her hands on top of the wood rail. "How are you doing, Curly?" she asked the new addition.

The piglet was the same age as Arnold's piglets and, she hoped, would fit in faster than another piglet might. It all depended on Arnold's feelings on the matter. Darby reached into her pocket and took out her last apple half, extending it through the slats. Arnold waddled over, sniffed then gobbled the snack up, her wet nose giving Darby's hand another pass. Darby stroked her fingers over her snout. "You'll take care of Curly, won't you, girl?" She glanced at the piglet cowering in the corner.

She kept stroking Arnold's snout, her own piglets contenting themselves with checking out the freshly laid straw. She noticed Curly step forward, then fall back again.

"Come on, baby," Darby quietly encouraged.

Arnold looked toward the orphan and gave a snort, sending the piglet scrambling back for the corner.

Darby frowned and glanced at her watch. She'd come out in a little while to check in on things. If Curly still hadn't approached Arnold, and Arnold hadn't welcomed her, then she'd be forced to bottle-feed the munchkin again.

Darby brushed her hands on her jean-clad thighs, shoved her hair back and headed out of the barn, closing the door after herself.

"Don't move."

Darby wasn't sure if it was the words themselves or the menacing way they were said, but she did exactly as she was told, freezing in her tracks. She felt fingers snake around the back of her neck, and a lump of fear so thick she could barely swallow filled her throat. Things like this didn't happen in Old Orchard. They only happened on television and in the movies, and even then in big cities. The lack of crime was what made smaller towns so appealing.

*Oh, my God, the girls!*

Darby glanced anxiously around. All she saw were two men in orange jumpsuits with O.O. Sheriff's Office stenciled over the one breast pocket. The girls were nowhere in sight.

She briefly closed her eyes, knowing that these two men were who John had been searching for the past three days. It struck her as ironic that they should show up at the very house John was staying in. Or was it by design? She wasn't sure which prospect scared her more.

"What do you want?" she asked, taking some comfort in knowing that they didn't have the girls. For once, she was grateful that the twins hadn't listened to her and had gone somewhere out of sight. She only hoped they didn't come barreling around the corner and straight into the situation.

The man holding her neck looked her up and down. "Hmm, I don't know. We were going to go into the barn when you happened to come out. Now all sorts of possibilities are presenting themselves."

"Are you alone?" the other man asked gruffly.

She swallowed. "My husband is out in the field."

A lie to be sure, but she also would have been lying had she said she was alone and they found the girls.

"You're not wearing a ring."

"I never wear a ring when I clean out the animal stalls. I touch all sorts of nasty things and I don't want to get it dirty."

The fingers on her neck increased their pressure. "You just violated the first rule in the con man's handbook. Never explain more than you have to. The longer the answer, the greater the chances it's a lie."

Darby shuddered, not liking his hand on her.

She licked her dry lips, knowing that with each

second that passed, the greater the chance the girls would show up. And she wanted, no, needed to prevent that from happening. ''Are you hungry? There's plenty of food in the house. I could, um, make you something to eat.''

The other man leaned toward the one holding her. ''The sheriff won't be out for long. He's sure to check here when he comes to.''

His words made her tremor. John was injured? She raised a hand as if to keep her heart from beating through her chest.

''We have a little time,'' the man holding her said. ''Let's see what Mrs....''

''Conrad,'' she supplied, her stomach tightening.

He leaned in closer to her and took a deep breath. ''Let's see what Mrs. Conrad has in mind for us inside.''

Inside. Inside there were all sorts of things she could do. All sorts of things she could use as a weapon.

But against two men?

He roughly turned her around and pushed her toward the house. ''Lead the way.''

Darby's gaze darted around the rest of the farm, searching for signs of the girls. There was none. She only hoped it would stay that way.

And she prayed John would make it there before the two men did even one of the things they might have in mind....

## Chapter Fourteen

*Keep them out in the open, Darby,* John silently pleaded. *Whatever you do, don't take them into the house.*

They were heading toward the house.

John cursed and got out of his Jeep. He'd parked it on the other side of the barn, out of sight of the two fugitives. His having a vehicle while they were on foot was the only thing he'd had going for him. But he was too late. They'd beaten him to Darby's farm.

He stumbled and grabbed the side of the Jeep. His head hurt like hell and he had yet to fully regain his equilibrium. He fisted his hands, willing himself to full capacity. He needed to have his wits about him if he had any hope of saving Darby.

Then there were the girls.

Were they in the house? What would Lyle and Ted Smythe do when they stumbled across them? He hadn't read anything on either of their rap sheets to indicate they were sexual predators or had a history of sexual assaults. But should they learn of Darby's connection to him, there was no telling what they might do.

On the wild drive over, he'd made a call to Ed and told him to send every available man out. Now he called to tell him that the fugitives were, in fact, there and that his backup should proceed with caution and meet him behind the barn.

That still left John with untold minutes until anyone else arrived. And, damn it, he couldn't just stand around and do nothing while those two scumbags were heading to the house with Darby.

John considered his options, finding them horribly lacking. He could confront the convicts now, without help, and risk them hurting Darby. Though he didn't see either of them holding a gun, he knew they had Ed's somewhere. So that meant that he didn't have the advantage of firepower. Unless in their rushed departure from the Jenkins place they'd left the gun behind. Even if they had, how much did that mean when one of them had his filthy paw around Darby's neck?

Okay, John thought. He could try a diversionary tactic and hope it stopped them from going inside.

He glanced around, his gaze settling on the chicken coop.

The chickens made such a ruckus that Darby gasped.

*The girls,* she immediately thought.

The man holding her by the neck whipped around to face the barn. She'd had her hand on the door handle, and the movement nearly tore her arm from the socket. She gave a soft yelp.

"What's that?" he demanded.

"It's, um, the chickens," she said quietly. "I have a coop on the other side of the barn."

They all stood for long minutes staring in the direction of the barn. Then the one holding her nudged his cohort with his elbow. "Go check it out, Ted."

"I'm sure everything's fine," Darby said quickly, afraid that the twins had riled the chickens. "They do that...all the time."

Both men stared at her.

"I'm not lying to you. Do you know much about farms?" She prayed they didn't. "If you do, then you know that chickens are high-maintenance creatures. Any little thing sets them off. The wind blows the wrong way and they kick up a fuss. Irritating as hell."

The one holding her grinned. "Check it out, Ted." He pulled Darby closer. "You couldn't lie to save your life, could you, Mrs. Conrad?"

Darby's blood ran cold. Was that what was at stake? Her life? What about the twins' lives if she allowed the other man to reach the barn?

"Come on," the man holding her said, turning her back toward the door. "Ted can take care of himself. I, on the other hand, am hungry as a horse. You'd better be a good cook. And having a little cash around wouldn't hurt, either. We didn't find a stinking penny at that damn house."

Darby's hand shook as she opened the door and stepped inside.

She realized her mistake the instant they both stood in the kitchen. Outside, where there was so much space, escape seemed possible. But inside she felt trapped, closed in.

What had she been thinking when she'd initially come up with the idea to entice the men inside?

The man finally released his grip on her neck, and she stumbled toward the counter, grasping the edge to reorient herself. Now that she was there, her mind went blank. The silverware drawer might be mere inches from her fingers, but did she dare pull a knife? Her right hand automatically sought her belly and the innocent life growing within.

The fugitive dropped into one of the kitchen chairs. Darby found it ironic that he chose the one in which John always sat.

*John.*

It hurt to think about him lying unconscious out there somewhere, injured by these two creeps. Would he be all right? Would he come to? Did someone, besides the two cons, know where he was?

"Get moving," the man behind her ordered, making her jump. "It's been a while since I've had a good home-cooked meal. The stuff they served at that jail wasn't fit for a dog." The chair legs screeched against the tile as he made himself more comfortable. "And don't get any bright ideas. You try to run, I'll only make things harder for you, if you get my meaning."

Darby forced herself to take the skillet out of the oven and place it on a burner. She eyed the heavy cast iron, wondering if she could knock him out with it. Fear gripped her. The pan was so heavy, she was afraid she wouldn't get halfway to the table before he'd see the attack coming.

Instead, she took a carton of fresh eggs out of the refrigerator. What to do…what to do…

"Now that's what I'm talking about," the man said, nodding in approval. "Sunny-side up. Do you know how to make hash browns? Been a while since I've had any of those."

Darby swallowed when she saw him spot one of the girl's dolls on the table. His expression hardened further as he picked the toy up by its hair, staring at it as if it were alive. "What's this?"

Darby's knees nearly gave out from under her. "My niece was over for a visit yesterday. She must have left it here."

Too long of an explanation? Would he recognize the lie for what it was? She began peeling potatoes like a fiend, watching as the skins dotted the stainless-steel sink. Out of the corner of her eye she saw him toss the doll back across the table and settle in to watch her.

She was so relieved a sob nearly ripped from her throat.

*Please, please, don't let his partner find the girls.*

Her gaze skittered to the door. Where was the guy? If she could disable this one, could she do the same with the other?

The fugitive went down like a ton of bricks.

John leaned back against the Jeep and stared at one

very unconscious Ted Smythe sprawled across the dusty earth. He tossed the nightstick he'd used to the hood, then extracted his cuffs from the back of his belt. Within seconds he had the guy bound to one of the metal poles supporting the chicken wire, ignoring the sound of the agitated chickens inside.

His gaze flicked to the front of the house some hundred yards away. One down, one to go.

He glanced at his watch, wondering how long it would take Cole and the others to get here. The problem was, he needed them out here now, while he still had the jump on the one inside the house with Darby. He had a unique edge what with one of the twosome out of commission. But he wouldn't have that edge for long. Lyle would figure out something was going on if his brother didn't return right away. And the element of surprise would be lost to him. And put Darby at even greater risk.

Stepping to the Jeep, he fished a roll of duct tape from his toolbox in the back, then taped the unconscious man's mouth shut. No sense taking a chance that he'd come to and try to warn his brother.

That done, John unsheathed his revolver and inched his way around the barn until he stood at the end of it. For the next stretch he'd be in the open where anyone looking out the window would be able to see him. Was Lyle at the kitchen door awaiting his brother's return? Chances were he was. But John didn't see any alternative.

He dragged the back of his left hand across his forehead, finding it drenched in sweat. His ears were still ringing from the blow to his head, and it was a battle to keep himself upright. The pain was intense. He didn't know what they had hit him with, but whatever it was had done more damage than he had the time to explore. But his concern about that was nothing compared to the frightening realization that Darby and the twins were in danger.

*Keep it together, man. Keep it together.*

He squinted against the late-afternoon sunlight, then made a visual inventory of the area to his right. The outside pen was about ten feet wide and twenty feet long, and contained the myriad animals Darby was renowned for having taken in. John blinked, finding Billy the Goat standing closest to him, chewing on Lord knows what and probably salivating over the chance to get his teeth on his hair again.

Glancing toward the house, John crouched as far down as he could, then followed the wooden railing to the gate. He released the latch and ducked inside, leaving the gate open. To his chagrin, the animals seemed more interested in him than in getting outside.

''Go on! Shoo!'' he said as loudly as he dared, swatting the llama on her hindquarters, then chasing the goat.

Finally the animals made for the gate. Using the diversion, John scrambled first next to the goat, then the llama, until he was very near the back door of the house, his heart beating erratically in his chest. He gripped his revolver tightly in both hands and pulled in several deep breaths. If he'd been spotted, there was no telling what Lyle would do.

He stood very still for long moments, waiting for

any sign that he'd been seen. Nothing. He felt a rush of relief, but quickly pushed it aside.

Okay, now what?

Since the guy he'd cracked on the head on the other side of the barn didn't have Ed's revolver, it stood to reason that Lyle did. Which meant that bursting through the door and ordering him to freeze wouldn't be the brightest of ideas.

Instead, he sidled up to the window over the kitchen sink and crouched just beneath it, wishing like hell his backup would hurry up and get there.

Darby shoved the potato peels down the drain, then flicked the wall switch to start the disposal. She was staring out the window, surreptitiously looking for the twins, when she spotted a fraction of a male head just below the window. She started, her heart nearly beating straight out of her chest.

*John.*

She couldn't imagine how he'd known to come here, but she was so relieved that he was she nearly fell over backward.

*The other guy's outside,* she tried to mentally convey to him. *And the twins are somewhere out there with him.*

"Hey. What's going on?"

The fugitive had gotten up from the table and stood right behind her. John's head disappeared.

"I almost dropped the knife into the disposal," she said, her voice shaking.

He squinted at her, then leaned across the sink to look out the window. Darby held her breath, hoping against hope that John had caught on to what was happening and had moved from his spot.

The convict looked at her again, then moved to the side door, staring in the direction of the barn.

"What's taking Ted so goddamn long?"

Darby picked up a metal spatula, then turned the browning shredded potato and onion patties in the skillet, hoping that his question was rhetorical and didn't require a response from her.

He glanced toward the stovetop and the food cooking there, then back at the barn.

"Turn it off."

Darby blinked at him. "What?"

"I said turn off the food." He stepped a little closer, his size alone menacing. "We're going outside to see what's happening."

Darby's throat made a clicking sound as she swallowed. "Maybe he's getting some fresh eggs?" she ventured.

"Ted wouldn't know a chicken from swine." He grabbed her arm. "Come on."

Darby scrambled to shut off the burners, then stumbled toward the door when he pushed her. Something cold and hard jabbed her side. She looked down to see what it was and gasped. From out of seemingly nowhere he had produced a silver six-shooter, fully cocked, his thumb on the trigger, the muzzle poking directly into her side.

"One wrong move, and you're history," he breathed into her ear.

The two outside steps seemed to hover in front of her, but she somehow managed to navigate them, her feet hitting hard earth. *John, please see the gun. Please.*

A metallic click sounded. Darby squeezed her eyes shut, sure she was about to die. Her hands immediately sought her stomach, trying helplessly to protect the tiny life within.

"Don't move," a hard voice she barely recognized ordered.

*John.*

Darby went completely limp. The hand gripping her arm tightened and she yelped in pain.

"Let her go."

The fugitive moved slightly, allowing John to see the gun he held to Darby's side.

John cursed, but didn't waver from where he held his own revolver pressed against the fugitive's temple.

"You shoot, she comes with me," the fugitive said, and Darby believed him. He actively eyed the barn area.

"Who are you looking for, Lyle?" John asked. "Your brother?" The questions earned him the guy's attention. "That's right. I put him out of commission the minute he came around the barn. And I fully intend to do the same to you."

The man pressed the gun into her side harder, and Darby gasped.

John stood as solid as a metal pole, one hand holding his firearm, the other clenching and unclenching.

Tires spitting gravel sounded. Darby jerked her head to see what was probably every law-enforcement vehicle in a fifty-mile radius turn into her driveway, coming from both the east and the west, clogging the two-lane road, sirens blaring, lights flashing.

The man holding her backed toward the house, taking her with him.

"Tell me, Lyle, what would make you head back to the Jenkins place after all that went down?"

The fugitive grinned, a sinister gesture that sent bumps scattering across Darby's skin. "I liked the scenery."

"Bullshit."

Darby remembered the piece she'd read following Violet's death. "Oh, my God. You went looking for the money she reportedly stashed somewhere in the house, didn't you?"

John cussed vividly. "Is that true?"

Lyle's black grin never wavered. "My brother and I wanted to escape the abuse we were suffering at your lockup, sheriff. Nothing more. Nothing less."

"Too much information," Darby whispered, knowing that it was true. Somehow the two convicts had heard the rumor about Violet Jenkins's estate and had scouted it out.

"Didn't find anything, did you?" John asked.

The grin turned into more of a scowl, and his grip on Darby became painful.

"That's because there is nothing to find." John's gaze latched on to Darby's for the first time since he'd accosted Lyle. In the hazel depths Darby saw fear, anxiety and so much love she suddenly found it difficult to swallow. He seemed to be trying to tell her something.

"Mommy!"

Oh, God, no!

Darby watched the twins being spit from the front of the barn and rushing toward them, apparently thinking everything was okay with the arrival of the cavalry.

Later, Darby would mentally work out what happened, but that moment she couldn't have said who made the first move. John grabbed her as he threw a kick to the back of Lyle's legs. A gunshot sounded and Darby felt the grip on her arm release. But all she could think of was getting to her girls. She ran in their direction, trying to shield them with her body, then dropped to her knees, her eyes widening suddenly as scorching fire ripped through her side. The same side that Lyle had had the gun pressed to.

Lindy and Erin catapulted into her arms. She caught them just before she fell backward onto the ground.

''Anything yet?''

John grabbed an intern hurrying through the doors of the emergency room. The young woman shook her head. ''No. No word yet, Sheriff. Sorry.''

John jammed his fingers into his hair and resumed pacing the hospital hall.

Two hours had passed since the ambulance attendants had wheeled Darby behind those cold metal doors. Two hours of sheer torture. Of thinking the worst. Praying for the best. And being left completely in the dark as to her condition.

Damn it to hell, she'd looked like death itself lying against the sheets, blood soaking through the gauze the paramedics kept pressed to her side. He remembered thinking that no one could lose that much blood and survive.

She'd been so still.

"Here, John. Drink this."

It took him a moment to realize someone had said something, then another to register who it was. He blinked to where Jolie was gently pressing a bottle of vending-machine orange juice into his hand, closing his fingers around it as if they were incapable of the movement without her help. He looked beyond her to where Darby's mother, Adelia, sat with the twins and Ellie in the glass-enclosed waiting area to his right.

"You're just getting in the way out here," Jolie said, steering him toward the room. "Come on. Wait with us in here."

John dug in his heels, staring at the twins' tear-streaked cheeks as they stared back at him. Their faces were white with fear. For the second time in their young lives they were faced with the prospect of losing a parent. And he felt he was to blame.

But Jolie Conrad hadn't been a firefighter for seven years, now chief, without knowing a few strength maneuvers. John was forced to enter the stale-smelling room. Jolie released him and he dropped into the plastic molded chair closest to the door, with a dead-on view of those cold metal doors at the end of the hall.

What had he done?

He dropped his head into his hands, his fingers biting into his closed eyes as he warded off a flood of emotion so strong he was dizzy with it.

One moment, he'd seen the outcome of an iffy situation gone bad, then the next, things had gotten even worse. He rocked slightly. He hadn't even known Darby had been shot until one of the twins, Lindy he thought, had cried out, blood staining her hands.

How could he not have known? How could he have done something he thought would help Darby, only to hurt her?

Please, God, let her make it through this.

He realized that in all his thoughts since arriving at the hospital, he hadn't thought about the baby she was carrying once. All he could think about was her. His love for Darby. His need that she be all right.

He felt a small, cold hand on his arm. "Don't worry. It's going to be all right."

John slowly slid his hands down his face and blinked into Erin's somber, angelic features.

Lindy appeared next to her sister and began patting his knee, her dark eyes wide. "You'll see. The doctor will make her all better. I know he will. Then we can all go home."

*Home.*

The reversal of their roles struck John. He, the adult, falling apart in an emergency room chair; they, the children who should be in need of comfort, instead comforting him.

He was so filled with gratitude that he nearly wept. He gathered both girls into his arms, then buried his face in their sweet-smelling hair. They felt so good, so right, cradled in his arms. He'd loved them from the day they were born. But as an uncle. Until now. Now he couldn't imagine loving them more had they been born his own children. And how very, very much he loved their mother. How he loved the baby she carried.

So much rested on what was happening in the other room it took his breath away.

He didn't know what he would do if he lost her. He refused even to consider the possibility. She had to pull through. She had to. For him. For the twins. For their baby.

"Shh," Lindy said, softly patting his shoulder. "Don't cry. Erin and me are here for you."

John pulled back, cupping both of their precious faces in his hands. He tried for a smile. "God, how I've missed you two."

This time when he hugged them, they hugged him back. John found himself thinking that Darby would have been happy about that. His eyes shut. Correction. She *would* be happy about that.

## Chapter Fifteen

Darby's mouth felt like someone had stuffed a roll of cotton into it. She tried to swallow, but got nothing but air.

"She's coming to," a soft female voice said. "Here, sweetheart. Open your mouth."

Darby did as asked and was rewarded with something cold and wet. Ice, she realized, as she tried but failed to open her eyes. It felt as though ten-pound weights rested on her eyelids.

"You're going to be okay. Right as rain," the female voice continued. "And so is your baby."

Darby seemed to be drifting on a fluffy white cloud, buoyed by the woman's words, yet unable to thank her.

"Darby?"

Even if her mind hadn't registered the sound of John's voice, the leap of her heart would have told her. Darby tried for a smile, then licked her lips. So dry.

Finally she pried her eyes open, but it took her a moment to focus. The instant she did, she gazed on the man who was not just the focal point of her eyes, but of her life.

She already knew that somewhere down the line, while fighting for exactly the opposite, she had fallen in love with Sheriff John Sparks. She just hadn't realized how deeply. So deeply she was afraid she no longer knew where she ended and he began. She felt him in her bones. In every breath she took. And every reason she'd conjured up to prevent them from taking their relationship to the next natural level fell away, leaving her with a knowing that nearly overwhelmed her.

"I'm so sorry," he whispered, taking her hand and lifting it to his mouth. He dragged his lips across her skin, leaving a trail of shivers in their wake. "I'm so very, very sorry."

She didn't know what he was apologizing for. Even without the nurse telling her, she knew her baby, their baby, was okay. She felt the baby's life force emanate from within, only reinforcing her love for the man looking more broken than she felt.

"Mommy!"

Darby swung her gaze from John's face to the twins, who bounded into the room, freeing themselves from Jolie's grip and racing for the bed. John caught them. "Careful. Mommy has to heal a bit before she's up for any jumping on the bed."

He easily hoisted them into his arms, both girls looking at him with gratitude, then at Darby.

Lindy leaned forward so that she could gently touch Darby's arm. "Are you okay, Mommy?"

Darby smiled. She caught Lindy's fingers and gave a reassuring squeeze. "I'm going to be fine, baby. Just fine. You wait and see."

Darby took in their beautiful faces, then looked at John again. Along with the baby in her womb, these were the most important people in her life. And she would never, ever, forget that.

"What's say we go get Mommy some ice cream?" Jolie's voice sounded behind John.

Darby looked at her dear friend gratefully. Jolie gave her a smile and a wink.

"That's sounds like a great idea," John said confidently, although his expression looked anything but confident.

Darby braced herself, expecting the girls to argue with him, to say they hated ice cream, anything to prevent their removal from the room. But instead, the twins grinned at him and nodded. "Okay," Erin said, allowing John to put her down. "Do you want some, too?"

John grinned. "Yeah. Ice cream sounds pretty good right now. I could go for some chocolate."

"Chocolate." Lindy nodded. "My favorite, too."

Jolie steered the girls through the door. Darby waved languidly at them, waiting until the door closed to look back at John.

"Am I imagining things, or did something happen while I was out?" she asked, her voice sounding reedy to her own ears.

John's grin warmed her to her toes. "Let's just say that I think we've declared a truce."

Darby sank back a little more comfortably against the pillows and gingerly smoothed her hand over the part of her belly that wasn't throbbing. She could feel the thick bandage on her left side covering her from just below her ribs to her hip. "Good. That means that everything's perfect, then."

John's grin vanished. "How can you say that?" he whispered. "I nearly got you—and our baby— killed."

She shook her head, love burgeoning in her heart. "Oh, no, John. You saved our lives."

He averted his gaze and she reached out to take his hands, refusing him escape.

"You can't have known what Smythe would have done if you hadn't moved when you did."

"It couldn't be worse than what he did do."

She ran her fingertips over his hands. Such strong, powerful hands. Capable of so much. And that he was unaware of their strength only added to his appeal. "Yes, it could have. I could be dead."

The stricken look on his face nearly made her smile.

"John," she said, tugging on his hands and forcing him to look at her. Really look at her. "I'm going to be okay. Our baby's going to be okay." She swallowed. "We're all going to be okay."

He squinted at her as if trying to read her thoughts.

She smiled and cleared her throat. "May I have some more ice, please?"

"Ice? Yes, ice," he said, appearing anxious as he grabbed for the plastic pitcher next to the bed. He lifted a few ice shavings to her mouth, his own opening as he did. She smiled and sucked the ice chips in.

"Thanks." She swallowed. "I don't know that I'm up for ice cream. You may have to help me out there."

"I'll help you with anything."

"I know."

Again that puzzled expression flickered across his face. His handsome, wonderful, unforgettable face.

She tried to smooth back her hair, imagining that she looked a mess. But somehow she couldn't make herself care.

She tried to choose her words carefully. Such an occasion deserved her best attention. When John reached for the pitcher again, she caught sight of the bandage at the back of his head.

"Oh, John, you were really hurt!" she whispered, reaching out to pull him closer.

He grimaced and caught her hand in his. "Compared to you, what happened to me was nothing."

"No. I know you were knocked unconscious by those men, and—"

He appeared suddenly agitated. "Damn it, woman, will you forget how I am? This isn't about me. You're the one lying in a hospital bed with a hole in her side."

She shook her head slowly, holding his gaze captive. "This isn't about me, either, John. It's about us."

John was two seconds away from moistening Darby's lips with his tongue and kissing her until she stopped skirting around what she was trying to say and just said it.

"There she is," Dr. Tucker O'Neill said as he breezed into the room, clipboard in hand.

John bit back the desire to ask the young doctor where else he expected Darby to be.

Tuck seemed completely oblivious to John as he stepped to the other side of the bed and checked Darby's pulse, then smiled his infamous Tuck smile at her. John had always hated Tuck. Well, okay, not hated. But he had always envied his blond good looks and his easy way with people. Especially women. All the guys did.

"How do you feel?" Tuck asked Darby.

"I think I'm going to live." She smiled back at him, and John felt a spark of jealousy. Which was dumb. He knew in his gut that he had nothing to fear. Yet when Tuck reached out and placed his hand on her abdomen, John had to use every shred of self-control he possessed to keep from launching himself across the bed.

"She's fine," John ground out.

Tuck met his gaze, looked startled, then removed his hand. "Good. Very good." He returned his attention to Darby, who was now smiling at John. "You had us all scared there for a while."

"What, with the best doctor in all of Ohio looking after me? Death never stood a chance."

Tuck's lips twisted. "Yes, well, just so long as you're okay."

John shifted his weight from foot to foot. "Is that all, Tuck?"

"All?" The doctor looked from John to Darby, then back to John, finally seeming to catch on that he'd walked in on something private. "Oh!" He flipped his chart closed and tucked it under his arm. "Guess I'll just go now," he said, and turned toward the door. "I'll check back later, okay?"

"Okay," Darby said.

"Fine. Great," John practically growled.

As soon as the door shut behind Tuck, Darby laughed softly. "What was all that about?"

John waved toward the hall distractedly. "Would you forget him? I want to know what you were about to say."

"Say?" she asked, looking far too innocent.

"Yes, say. You referred to everything being perfect. That this moment wasn't about you or me, but us," he prompted.

"Right," she said then made a production out of straightening the bed covers.

"So…?"

She lifted her gaze. "I have only one word to say to you, John."

He suddenly found it difficult to swallow. Uh-oh. Here it was. She was going to give it to him but good for having played the hotshot today and gotten her injured, putting her through a prolonged operation and what were sure to be endless weeks of recuperation.

"What?" he forced himself to ask.

She licked her lips, looking beyond him to the door. The same door the girls would be bouncing through any second.

"Darby…" he said, his voice holding a warning.

The smile she bestowed on him was so bright he nearly had to blink against it. "Yes."

He didn't get it. That was the one word she had for him? Yes? Yes, as in what? Yes, he was to blame for everything that had happened today? Yes, the girls would be returning any minute? Yes, he was an idiot for ever thinking himself deserving of her?

She didn't offer more. Merely lay there looking like an angel and smiling at him as if waiting for him to get the point.

"Yes, what?"

Again she laughed softly. "The answer to your question. You know, the one you were waiting for?" She searched his eyes. "Yes," she whispered.

His question…

John's heart skipped a beat as he remembered what question she was talking about. The only question still outstanding between the two of them. A question he'd asked repeatedly, receiving the same answer, until the morning they'd made love for the first time in her bed and she hadn't answered at all.

Until now.

She was saying yes to his marriage proposal.

"Oh, baby," he murmured, carefully sliding his fingertips over her cheekbones, then into the tangle of soft brown hair. He pressed his lips gingerly against hers, drinking in everything that was Darby Parker Conrad, soon to be Sparks.

She moved her hand to the back of his head, feeling the bandage there, then lowered her fingers to his neck, pulling him closer. "I got shot in the side, you moron, not the head. Kiss me like you mean it."

He grinned and did exactly as she asked.

## *Epilogue*

*Six months later*

A girl. They'd been blessed with a baby girl.

John stood back from Darby's hospital bed in the special suite in the hospital birthing unit and gaped at his wife and new daughter, at a loss for words. Hell, at a loss for much of anything. All he could do was just stand there and stare.

That that pink, wrinkled, wriggling little package had his blood running through her veins seemed incredible. And incredibly magical.

"Daddy?" Darby said softly.

"Huh?" He looked into her face, finding it even more remarkable that the woman holding his baby, their baby, was his wife.

"Do you want to hold her?"

John's eyebrows hiked up to his hairline. "Hold...her?" He motioned helplessly and took a step back. Then another. "You don't think I'll hurt her? She's so tiny. So fragile." *So female.*

John scrubbed the back of his neck with his hand. At some point this morning, as family and friends poured into the birthing suite bearing little pink booties, frilly dresses and dolls—lots of dolls—John was overwhelmed by the odds lengthening against him. Four to one is how it now stood. Darby, the twins and now their latest addition. Four females to his one male.

Oh, boy.

"Trust me, you won't break her," Darby said, holding the little pink bundle out to him.

"I wouldn't be so sure."

It wasn't all that long ago that he'd "broken" Darby by pulling a fast one on Smythe that ended up in her being shot.

He took a hesitant step forward. Then another. Until with shaking hands he reached for the oh-so-quiet baby.

"She's so light," he remarked softly, staring in wonder at the small human being in his hands. He moved to lay her first one way, then the other in his arms, then gave up and rested her against his shoulder. So tiny. So warm. He stroked a finger down one of her cheeks. So very, very soft.

Darby laid her hand against his, her wedding ring throwing off shafts of light. No matter how much water she retained, she'd refused to take the ring off. At one point Tuck had threatened to have it cut off. She'd told him he'd have to take her finger with it if he even got near her with a saw.

"So, Sheriff Sparks, what are we going to name our new addition?" Darby asked softly.

They'd batted around several names for either sex for months. But now that John held this precious little girl in his arms, none of the names they'd come up with seemed to fit. Except for one.

He met Darby's gaze. "I don't know."

She smiled. "Why don't we let her tell us, then?"

"Can you do that? I thought we had to decide on a name now—you know, for the birth certificate."

Darby waved her hand. "Let me worry about that."

He narrowed his gaze on her. "You're not suggesting we break the law, are you?"

She shook her head. "No. Merely bend it a little." She smoothed the blanket across her abdomen, looking spectacularly sexy even in her cotton nightgown. Especially in her cotton nightgown, her breasts full. "Besides, you won't be sheriff for much longer."

John waited for the shock of that statement to hit him, but standing there looking at his beautiful wife and holding his new beautiful daughter, the prospect of hanging up his sheriff's cap seemed insignificant, indeed.

Truth was, he was happy to be moving on. To be handing over the reins to Cole, who was sure to win against the opportunist Bully Wentworth. John planned to throw his full support behind his colleague. And considering his herolike status after apprehending the escaped fugitives, the preelection polls already showed Cole holding a 2-1 lead.

Sometime after the same incident that had earned him hero status, John had come to realize that some things were more important. Like his family. He and Darby had expanded The Promised Land farm, secured grants for the running of it, and he was studying to become a full-time farmer. He didn't kid himself into thinking it would be smooth sailing. And Darby had agreed to his being an alternate firefighter, but he felt the rightness of his decisions clear down to his bones.

The little bundle in his arms coughed a couple of times, then let out a wail that nearly broke his eardrums. John held her out, staring at her in horror, without a clue of what to do.

Darby laughed softly. "That'll work."

John looked beyond his crying daughter. "I think you should take her."

Darby shook her head. "I think she's just fine where she is. Try holding her close again. In the crook of your arm so she can see you."

How was he supposed to do that when the kid was wailing like a banshee? He awkwardly did as Darby demonstrated, then almost immediately the newborn stopped crying, instead, staring up at him with apparently as much wonder as he was staring at her.

"There you go," Darby whispered. "Why do I get the feeling that this one's going to be Daddy's little girl?"

John grinned, suddenly feeling ten feet tall and more important than he'd ever felt as sheriff.

* * *

"You can go faster than five miles an hour, John."

He looked at Darby where she sat in the passenger seat of the Jeep smiling at him, then glanced back to where their daughter was experiencing her first car ride. Home. He could barely make her out with the infant seat facing toward the back seat.

He cleared his throat. "This will only happen one time. I intend to enjoy every minute of it."

He noticed Darby's shiver. She was likely remembering another time when he'd set out to thoroughly enjoy a moment out of time. Their wedding night.

Neither of them could think of a single place they'd rather be than at the farmhouse alone together. And he'd taken advantage of every precious moment alone with this new wife. And welcomed the return of the twins early the next morning. But rather than glaring at them from their bedside, the twins had crawled into bed with them, one on either side.

Good thing one of their wedding presents had been a pair of pajamas for him.

The baby gave a couple of soft coughs, then started crying.

"Should I pull over to the side of the road?" he asked. "See what's the matter?"

Darby laughed. "You can't stop the car every time she cries, John."

He tightened his hands on the wheel and accelerated. Slightly. While he'd grown a little more accustomed to hearing his daughter cry, the sound never failed to flip some sort of protection switch within him that made him want to ban all pain from her young life.

"Sharon," Darby said.

John nodded, knowing she was continuing the name debate. They still hadn't decided on one. And since the newborn couldn't speak, she couldn't tell them what she preferred.

He quietly cleared his throat, wondering if now was the time to tell her what he had in mind.

"You don't like it?" Darby asked.

"Yes. Yes, it's nice." He paused. "But…well, I don't know. There's one name I keep coming back to."

Darby glanced at him. "I didn't know you had a favorite."

He swallowed. "Yes, well, I didn't want to say anything until I was sure. I didn't want to upset you."

"Why would a suggestion for a name upset me?"

He glanced at her. "Because the name is Erica."

*Erica.* He didn't have to say anything more.

In the back seat, the baby abruptly stopped crying and made a soft cooing sound, instead.

"I, um, understand if you don't want to, you know, name her that," he said when Darby remained silent.

He shifted uncomfortably, waiting for her response.

Ever since they'd first begun tossing around baby names, the name Eric for a boy or Erica for a girl had topped his list. But he wasn't sure how Darby would feel about naming their baby after her late husband. But Erick had been more than just her late husband to him. He had been his best friend. Closer to him than a brother. And he couldn't help wondering sometimes, late in the night when a breeze stirred the white sheers on their bedroom window, if Erick not only had a hand in his and Darby's getting together, but approved wholeheartedly of their union.

Naming their daughter Erica would bring everything full circle.

"Erica," Darby whispered. "Erica."

Finally she smiled. "I like it." She slid her hand across the seat and squeezed his thigh. "I like it a lot."

John experienced such intense gratitude he nearly pulled off the road to kiss her.

He settled for holding her hand. For now.

The farm appeared on the horizon.

Darby turned in her seat and tucked a blanket more tightly around the baby's chubby legs. "We're almost home, Erica. What do you think of that?"

John leaned forward. The nearer they drew to the farm, the more he sensed something different. "Who's going to be at the house besides your mom with the twins?"

Darby shrugged and looked out her window as if she wasn't concerned one way or the other. "I don't know." But John sensed that she did know. He caught her smile before she could completely turn away.

"Uh-huh."

John could make out at least five cars in the driveway. For all he knew, there were more parked next to the house, out of sight. He picked out several of his family members' cars, Cole's sheriff's vehicle and Dusty's truck.

"What in hell are they doing?" he asked under his breath, staring at where a large tarp had been draped across the side of the barn. And the remainder of the barn he could see was no longer gray, but a deep red.

"Can't say as I know," Darby said, not even trying to hide her smile now.

John pulled into the drive, forced to stop behind the line of other vehicles. He switched off the engine and climbed out, staring at the gathering of people near the barn.

"John! John!" Erin cried, covered from head to toe in what looked like white paint. Lindy followed on her heels.

The seven-year-olds launched themselves at him, and he crouched and caught them up in his arms. He turned toward where Darby was getting Erica out of her car seat, Jolie and a couple of his sisters helping her.

"Come over here, John," Lindy said, her face full of excitement. "Hurry."

John narrowed his gaze. "What have you two been up to since I left this morning?"

"You'll see," Erin said, tugging on his hand.

John allowed himself to be led to what he gathered was the predetermined stopping point. Dusty came up to stand beside him. "Congratulations, Sparky."

John grinned. "Yeah. Thanks."

Dusty grinned back, not needing to say anything more. As Erick's brother, Dusty knew better than anyone what all of them had gone through. And, black eye aside, had been one hell of a support.

Darby and the baby were crossed to John's other

side. He draped his arm over her shoulders and placed his free hand on Erin's soft head, where she stood with Lindy in front of him.

"Okay, guys, guess this is it," Dusty called out to John's brothers, who stood off to one side of the barn.

"No, no, no!" Erin cried. "The countdown, Uncle Dusty. You forgot the countdown."

John lifted his brows at his friend.

Dusty chuckled. "Okay. On the count of three, everyone."

"One…" everyone present said in unison, the girls' voices ringing out.

"Two…"

"Three!"

His older brother Ben pulled on a cord. Nothing.

John laughed, only to earn an elbow from Darby. "What?" he asked.

She nodded her head toward the barn.

When he hadn't been looking, the tarp had drifted to the ground to reveal the words THE SPARKS FAMILY spelled out in white letters as tall as his Jeep.

John gazed at his wife, feeling more love for her at that moment than he ever thought himself capable of feeling.

"I love you," she murmured.

He kissed her, reminding himself not to squash the baby still in her arms. He felt a hand tugging on his shirt.

"Us, too!" Lindy said.

John hiked them both up, then pulled Darby close again, holding all of his girls safely in his arms.

*   *   *   *   *

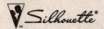

# SPECIAL EDITION™

### Coming in August 2002,
### from Silhouette Special Edition and

## CHRISTINE RIMMER,

the author who brought you the popular series

### *CONVENIENTLY YOURS,*

brings her new series

# THE SONS OF
# CAITLIN
# BRAVO

### Starting with

## HIS EXECUTIVE SWEETHEART
### (SE #1485)...

One day she was the prim and proper executive assistant...
the next, Celia Tuttle fell hopelessly in love with her boss,
mogul Aaron Bravo, bachelor extraordinaire. It was clear he
was never going to return her feelings, so what was a girl to
do but get a makeover—and try to quit. Only suddenly,
was Aaron eyeing his assistant in a whole new light?

And coming in October 2002, MERCURY RISING,
also from Silhouette Special Edition.

**THE SONS OF CAITLIN BRAVO: Aaron, Cade and Will.**
**They thought no woman could tame them.**
**How wrong they were!**

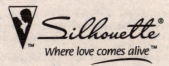

*Where love comes alive*™

If you enjoyed what you just read,
then we've got an offer you can't resist!

## Take 2 bestselling love stories FREE!
## Plus get a FREE surprise gift!

Clip this page and mail it to Silhouette Reader Service™

**IN U.S.A.**
3010 Walden Ave.
P.O. Box 1867
Buffalo, N.Y. 14240-1867

**IN CANADA**
P.O. Box 609
Fort Erie, Ontario
L2A 5X3

**YES!** Please send me 2 free Silhouette Special Edition® novels and my free surprise gift. After receiving them, if I don't wish to receive anymore, I can return the shipping statement marked cancel. If I don't cancel, I will receive 6 brand-new novels every month, before they're available in stores! In the U.S.A., bill me at the bargain price of $3.99 plus 25¢ shipping and handling per book and applicable sales tax, if any*. In Canada, bill me at the bargain price of $4.74 plus 25¢ shipping and handling per book and applicable taxes**. That's the complete price and a savings of at least 10% off the cover prices—what a great deal! I understand that accepting the 2 free books and gift places me under no obligation ever to buy any books. I can always return a shipment and cancel at any time. Even if I never buy another book from Silhouette, the 2 free books and gift are mine to keep forever.

235 SDN DNUR
335 SDN DNUS

| Name | (PLEASE PRINT) | |
| --- | --- | --- |
| Address | Apt.# | |
| City | State/Prov. | Zip/Postal Code |

\* Terms and prices subject to change without notice. Sales tax applicable in N.Y.
\*\* Canadian residents will be charged applicable provincial taxes and GST.
  All orders subject to approval. Offer limited to one per household and not valid to current Silhouette Special Edition® subscribers.
  ® are registered trademarks of Harlequin Books S.A., used under license.

SPED02                                    ©1998 Harlequin Enterprises Limited

Beloved author

# Joan Elliott Pickart

introduces the next generation
of MacAllisters in

## The Baby Bet:

### MacALLISTER'S GIFTS

with the following heartwarming romances:

**On sale September 2002**
**PLAIN JANE MacALLISTER**
Silhouette Desire #1462

**On sale December 2002**
**TALL, DARK AND IRRESISTIBLE**
Silhouette Special Edition #1507

And look for the next exciting installment
of the MacAllister family saga,
coming to Silhouette Special Edition in 2003.

*Don't miss these unforgettable romances…*
*available at your favorite retail outlet.*

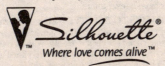

Silhouette®
*Where love comes alive*™

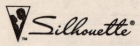

# COMING NEXT MONTH

### #1507 TALL, DARK AND IRRESISTIBLE—Joan Elliott Pickart
*The Baby Bet: MacAllister's Gifts*
From the moment they met, it was magic. But Ryan Sharpe and Carolyn St. John were both scarred by a lifetime of hurts. Then the two met an adorable little boy who desperately needed their help, and they realized that having the courage to face the past was their only hope for a future…together.

### #1508 THE COWBOY'S CHRISTMAS MIRACLE— Anne McAllister
*Code of the West*
Deck the halls with…romance? Widowed mom Erin Jones had loved lone wolf cowboy Deke Malone years ago, but he'd only seen her as a friend. Suddenly, the holidays brought her back into Deke's life…and into his arms. Would the spirit of the season teach the independent-minded Montana man that family was the best gift of all?

### #1509 SCROOGE AND THE SINGLE GIRL—Christine Rimmer
*The Sons of Caitlin Bravo*
Bubbling bachelorette Jillian Diamond loved Christmas; legal eagle Will Bravo hated all things ho-ho-ho. Then Will's matchmaking mom tricked the two enemies-at-first-sight into being stuck together in an isolated cabin during a blizzard! Could a snowbound Christmas turn Will's bah-humbug into a declaration of love?

### #1510 THE SUMMER HOUSE— Susan Mallery and Teresa Southwick
*2-in-1*
Sun, sand and ocean. It was the perfect beach getaway, and best friends Mandy Carter and Cassie Brightwell were determined to enjoy it…alone. But summers could be full of surprises. Especially when lovers, both old and new, showed up unexpectedly!

### #1511 FAMILY PRACTICE—Judy Duarte
High-society surgeon Michael Harper was the complete opposite of fun-loving cocktail waitress Kara Westin. Yet, despite their differences, Michael couldn't help proposing marriage to help Kara gain custody of two lovable tots. Would Michael's fortune and Kara's pride get in the way of their happily-ever-after?

### #1512 A SEASON TO BELIEVE—Elane Osborn
Jane Ashbury had been suffering from amnesia for over a year when a Christmas tune jarred her back to reality. With so much still unknown, private detective Matthew Sullivan was determined to help Jane piece together the puzzle of her past. And when shocking secrets started to surface, he offered her something better: a future filled with love!

SSECNM1102